Sweet Pear

JESSICA BUTLER

Sweet Pear
Copyright © Jessica Butler, 2021
All rights reserved.

Cover and Interior Design:: Jennie Lyne Hiott @ bookcoverit.com

ISBN: 9798479009648

Copyright inspires creativity, encourages the sharing of voices, and creates a vibrant civilization. Thank you for purchasing an authorized edition of this book and for complying with copyright laws by not reproducing, scanning, or distributing any part of it in any form, electronic or mechanical, without written permission from the author, except in the case of brief quotation embodied in critical articles and reviews.

This is a work of fiction. The names, characters, places, and incidents are products of the writer's imagination or are used fictitiously and should not be construed as real. Any similarities to persons, living or dead, actual events, locale or organizations is entirely coincidental.

Always Choose Bliss ♡

[signature]

For the amazingly strong women in my life who aren't afraid to ponder life's greatest questions through the eyes of non-judgment and love.

Contents

Prologue
Chapter One
Chapter Two
Chapter Three
Chapter Four
Chapter Five
Chapter Six
Chapter Seven
Chapter Eight
Chapter Nine
Chapter Ten
Chapter Eleven
Chapter Twelve
Chapter Thirteen
Chapter Fourteen
Chapter Fifteen
Chapter Sixteeen
Chapter Seventeen
Chapter Eighteen

Chapter Nineteen
Chapter Twenty
Chapter Twenty-One
Chapter Twenty-Two
Chapter Twenty-Three
Chapter Twenty-Four
Chapter Twenty-Five
Chapter Twenty-Six
Chapter Twenty-Seven
Chapter Twenty-Eight
Chapter Twenty-Nine
Chapter Thirty
Chapter Thirty-One
Chapter Thirty-Two
Chapter Thirty-Three
Chapter Thirty-Four
Acknowledgements

Prologue

This can't be happening. I'm in the bathroom splashing cold water from the faucet onto my face while also trying to pry my eyes open because I have to still be asleep. I'm sleeping, right? This is like one of those lucid dreams where you realize you're asleep so you have to either navigate what move you make or you wake the hell up. I'm choosing option number two because this feels too real for my liking.

After dramatically peeling open my eyes with my pointer fingers and thumbs and accidentally poking myself twice; I realize this isn't working. Suddenly, I hear a knock on the bathroom door. "Yeah?" I nervously call out.

"Babe, what are you doing in there? I have to take a piss." No doubt at all in that voice. I was right in who I saw lying next to me in bed. That voice does not belong to my husband, it's coming from my ex-boyfriend.

Chapter One

You know that feeling when your stomach drops and you can actually feel pain coarse through your body? That's currently happening to me. How is this possible?

"I'll be right out, give me a minute!" I manage to squeak out, before putting the toilet seat cover down and taking a seat. I glance around the room and try to regain my composure. It's then I notice; this isn't my bathroom. I'm not in my house. Am I having an affair? If I am, why can't I remember? Was I roofied? I don't think so; but who would know that? Why the hell am I at my ex's house and why is he calling me babe?

"OK", I say out loud to myself as I take a moment to pause. "Think Elle, think." My head is pounding and my mouth is dry. Those are classic signs of the next day hangover. I was definitely drinking last night. Maybe I can replay last night's events and quickly before he calls my name again. I'm forcing myself to think so hard and fuzzy memories start to enter. I was at a martini bar with my girlfriends having one of those monumental nights full of vent sessions where you realize maybe we should have just all stayed single and lived together instead of dealing with everyday life filled with work, paying bills, husband problems, baby problems, dating problems and then ... he walked in. There goes that stomach drop again.

I hear a knock on the door again. My thought bubble pops and I know in that moment what I need to do. I need to get out of here immediately and go see my best friend, Gwen. She'll help fill in the gaps for me. Ok Elle, here we go. Just get yourself out of the bathroom and proceed to the nearest exit. I stand up quickly and immediately have that dizzy feeling where you feel like you just got off of a treadmill. I take a few deep breaths and prepare to make my way to leave.

As I open the door, I come face to face with him. God, why does he always give me this feeling when we lock eyes. He's standing shirtless only wearing his boxer briefs and he looks good. His golden-brown hair is ruffled in a perfect "I woke up like this" concoction. "What's that look for?" he asks with his eyebrows furrowed. "Nothing, " I say quickly. "I have to go meet Gwen. So... umm nice to see you." "Nice to see you? " he laughs. "Ok nice to see you too Ellie, I'll see you again later tonight. Love ya." He goes to reach down to possibly kiss me but I dart under his arm. "Mm hmm" is all I can muster out before I'm able to locate my dress on the floor (one I haven't worn in ages by the way) and slip my feet into flats to sprint it outside.

As I walk outside, I inhale the biggest breath of air I can muster and hope this wakes me up. I open my eyes and am greeted with the same image as before. Alright, you're definitely not sleeping Elle. Time to get out of here! I start to speed walk down the driveway to my car while my mind spirals. Was he going to kiss me? Did he really say love ya? Why would he say that? If we were having a one-night stand or whatever this is, isn't that progressing a little too fast? I mean, Jesus when we dated it took him a year and a half before he could even mutter those words. Then a full four years before he could look me in the eyes and tell me he loved me but wasn't "in love" with me. So how exactly do we go from that to, whatever is going on right now.

Of course, I'm hitting every red light on the way and feel like my car can't get to Gwen's house quick enough. By the time I actually pull into her driveway, I realize I've been gripping the steering wheel so hard it has nail indentations.

SWEET PEAR

I know it's a little selfish of me to run up to her house unannounced when she has a house full of kids and a husband but if there's any time I can put in my phone a friend card it's now! As I'm running up her walkway, I stop to briefly admire her landscaping skills. I mean, I have zero kids and can't bother to water my aloe plant but she finds time in between taking care of four kids to be Susie Green thumbs? I crouch down to a beautiful display of long red flowers that I've only ever seen in Hawaii, like did she get them shipped here? I need to do better. Ok...refocus Elle, this is important, I tell myself as I stand up and continue towards the door. I ring the bell and realize I'm doing my pee dance, aka my nervous dance where I'm shifting weight from one foot to the other and swaying side to side. The door opens and little Madison opens it.

"Aunt Elle!" she shrieks and gives me the biggest hug, which is also sticky because it seems she's been eating some pancakes with her syrup today. "Hi sweetie, is mommy here? I ask with desperation while glancing nervously past her. "Yeah, she's inside; come on in!" she says as she does the best model sashay down the hall. How does a five-year-old have so much confidence? Is it something that's born with us and we lose it as we get older or is it just something a select few receive that they're always able to hold onto?

I'm running up behind Madison with speed like a shopping cart wheel about to hit her ankle when I see Gwen. She's in the kitchen with an apron tied around her. I mean c'mon now, do people still own aprons, let alone wear them? She turns around to start to say "What up girlllll" ... as she stops midway. I watch her scan me up and down as she quickly changes her tone saying, "Elle, what's wrong?" I repeat back her question almost instantly. "What's wrong? Hmmm. Well, I think I'm finally going crazy!" I try to say under my breath so I don't scare her children. "So, there's that!" I laugh nervously as I throw my hands up.

She places the spatula down on the counter and calmly calls out, "Greg, takeover parent time!" I watch her grab two adult sippy cups (don't judge) and fill them up to the top with prosecco. She then puts swirly straws in and hands me one. It's like she's been prepared and waiting for me to come in with this category 5 warning. "Gwen, it's 10 AM," I exclaim. "And your point is?" she questions. "Come on, let's walk and talk."

We step outside and walk along her driveway to the sidewalk as I think to myself how lucky I am to have a friend like Gwen. She's been my best homegirl since kindergarten when we walked up to each other at the swing set as if someone had their hands placed on our backs as they brought us to each other. I swear to God we just had this recognition we have been through this life before and how lucky we are to meet again. She's my person I know I can be my unedited self with and vice versa.

"So lay it on me," she says as she hands me her glass while putting her long silky, brown hair into a perfect top knot. "Ok so...I don't even know where to start. Umm first, I'm having problems remembering what exactly happened last night so I don't know if I was roofied or what; but all I know is I woke up in bed and turned over and the man next to me wasn't my husband."

"Oh...I wasn't expecting that. Wow...ok." Gwen says. I notice she takes a longer sip of her prosecco so I follow suit. "Ok", she repeats. "So, who is it? Wait, do you know who it is?"

"Yeah, I know who it is", I admit quietly as I nod. "That's what makes it even more difficult to say. Ok so please don't judge me." She then hits me on the shoulder. "Don't ever say that to me, of course I would never judge you," she states, followed by another long sip. "Ok here it goes", I say as I take a few deep breaths and mentally prepare for her reaction. "The person who was next to me in bed was, get ready for it ... Josh Wilson."

Gwen takes a moment and I'm bracing myself because I totally understand if she'd be confused. I mean, I'm confused and this is happening to me! I haven't seen him in years. I mean this guy basically destroyed me and messed with me in a way that I couldn't trust any man for a really long time, until I met Ryan. There was a period of weeks where I didn't even leave my house, except to go into work. My girlfriends literally showed up one day, led me to the shower, picked out clothes for me and hijacked me back out into the world of socialization. I know she's probably wondering how this started back up, and more importantly why? She finishes the rest of her prosecco and then wipes her mouth with the back of her hand. I watch her as she pauses and looks me dead in the eyes with a serious look on her face. She puts both hands on my shoulders and looks at me lovingly but there's also another emotion I can't place. It's almost as if she's a little frightened. "Elle, you're married to Josh Wilson."

Chapter Two

"Ok stop!" I laugh as I drink a little more prosecco until I realize she's not joking. "Ok...stop!" I yell. Gwen takes her hands off of my shoulders and says with tenderness in her voice, "Ok so tell me everything. You don't think you're married to Josh?" I yell out quickly, "No, Josh is my toxic ex-boyfriend who would always somehow bring me back to him but that's very far back into the past. I don't know how I ended up in his house, let alone his bed but I'm not married to him. I'm married to Ryan."

"Ok and who is Ryan?" she asks calmly. I know she probably thinks I'm legit crazy but I try not to get too worked up as I take a moment to collect my thoughts. "Alright so I'll give you the 101 cliff notes version to indulge you but Ryan is my husband. He's my rock, he's the guy I've been waiting for my whole life and he's amazing. I love him, you love him, I mean basically everyone loves him that meets him."

Gwen looks at me and I can see her brace herself so I know the next question is going to be difficult. "Ok Elle, don't get mad but if he's all that, then why did you wake up next to Josh?" It's a good question, I think to myself. I mean I can't even really answer it. We sit down on a nearby bench as I fill Gwen in on everything.

I tell her about our life together, group trips we have taken, our inside jokes and even our little chore chart I made so that we are both putting the same amount of work into our house and life. She is listening intently while also tilting her glass trying to find any droplets left of prosecco when I hand her mine to finish off. I know she has to think I'm insane. "Ok", she says. "I'll admit it; you sound a little insane, but I believe you. I mean I don't know what's going on but I totally buy something profound has happened so I'll help in any way I can." I can see she genuinely means this and isn't just trying to appease me. I give her the biggest hug (without the syrup) and wipe my tears away that have formed in the corner of my eyes.

"Ok first things first; check your phone and look for Ryan in your contacts", Gwen suggests. "Oh, good idea", I reply with enthusiasm. I scroll through my phone excitedly which quickly dissipates after seeing there's not one single Ryan in there. Not even friends named Ryan. "Ok wait! There's a babe in my contacts. That's got to be him! I'm calling." Gwen watches me as I perk up waiting to hear Ryan's voice and find out this was all just a massive prank that I don't find even remotely funny. It keeps ringing and ringing which I have to admit is bizarre because even if Ryan isn't free, he answers quickly and says "hey babe can't talk now" just as a common courtesy. I keep hearing the ringing and ringing and just as I'm about to hang up the voicemail pops on. "Hey, it's Josh. Clearly, I don't feel like talking or I'm doing something better where I can't answer so leave a message and if you're lucky, you'll hear from me." Then I hear his little chuckle followed by the recording beep. I quickly hang up and the blood rushes from my head.

I look up at Gwen and say, "Ok so I've completely lost it" as I can't hold it back any longer and start to cry. "Don't cry" Gwen says as she puts her arms around me and pulls out a trial size alcohol bottle and hands it to me. "I thought we may need this from the way you looked in my kitchen." I don't even know nor do I care what it is as I unscrew the cap and let the liquid go down followed by a familiar warmth.

"I just can't make sense of it", I say over and over as I place my hands over my face into my lap. If this is true, why am I not remembering it? Suddenly a realization hits me. "Oh my God, do I have children?" "No", Gwen let me know. "You weren't ready for that yet and I have to say that's a smart decision." "Ok good" I exhale with relief. "Wait, why?" I ask with curiosity. "Nothing, don't worry about that. That's not important right now" she says. "I'm not going to give any opinions except the facts so your brain doesn't get swirled with more confusion."

I ask if I could google Ryan to a.) Make sure he's a real person and b.) See if I'm in any of the pictures so I could slap a big old I told you so to Gwen. "Girl, I've been waiting for you to ask this because I want to see too" she says. "What's his last name though; you never told me." "Elverson" I say as I continue to look through my contacts list, seeing if I missed his name. She starts cracking up. "What?" I ask. "What's so funny about that?" "Oh, I don't know, maybe that you're telling me you actually agreed to have your name be Elle Elverson!" "Oh, that's right" I laugh. "It did take you a while to get over that, I remember." It used to be a funny thing where when we first got married, she'd giggle when she'd call me Mrs. Elle Elverson saying, "You just love yourself so much Elle you had to find someone with the last name that is basically your first." I have a moment of nostalgia of those first few years with Ryan where we were just so blissfully happy, couldn't get enough of each other mentally and physically. And then ... I'll wait to tell Gwen about that part. There's too much going on right now anyways for me to remember. As I sit there feeling all of the emotions, Gwen snaps me out of it.

"Ok, ummm is this him Elle?" She turns her phone towards me and there he is. My husband. He looks just as I remembered him but better. Distinguished maybe? "Yeah, there's Ryan. Aw he looks so good. So, what does it say about him? Is he married?" I ask with my heart beating out of my chest waiting for the answer. "Um ... hang on, let me take a look," she says. "Blah blah blah, boring, boring, boring ... Oh, Ohhhhhh!" she says and then I watch her eyes dart back and forth. She's reading but not vocalizing it.

"Gwen! C'mon what does it say? Stop hogging it for yourself." "OK! Well, I didn't realize this was him but Elle he's a pretty well-known chef. He has restaurants all over, it looks like. One in New York, Nashville, Chicago, Vegas and the original started right here which we've actually been to before." "Oh really? What's it called?" I ask as I grab the phone from her to look at him one more. "It's called Sweet Pear; do you remember that place? They have the best goat cheese toasts, mmmm I could totally go for one right now! They're perfectly crusty but also maintain that chewy center and they're freaking delicious." I hear her talking but I can't focus. My dizziness has returned and I'm feeling sweaty and cold at the same time. It's at this moment I actually do what I've been feeling needed to happen since I woke up next to Josh. I get up from the bench, turn and squat down low and throw up. Sweet Pear, he named the restaurants Sweet Pear. You see, that's the nickname Ryan gave to me the first night I met him.

Chapter Three

Hours later, after Gwen fed me and sobered me up (I can be a lightweight sometimes), I'm on my way back "home". I didn't want to come back to a place that feels so foreign but also so familiar to me. Josh is in the same home he was living in when we broke up. So much trauma and heartbreak happened at this place, why would I want to go back to it? Gwen told me it was important to act the part to him as everyone wouldn't be reacting the same way she did to my confession. Sweet Pear; that has to mean something, doesn't it? It can't just be a weird coincidence. I mean, what are the odds he would he name his restaurants the same name that he gave to me as a nickname the first night we met? God, I remember that night like it was yesterday.

I was out to dinner with the girls, as per usual, at this local pub that just so happens to make the most amazing sandwiches. It's basically the best place to go to for cheap drinks and food that also feeds your soul. Anyway, I remember all of it. I remember how Lizzie was telling us about one of her one-night stands that ended with the guy's cat peeing all over her new suede purse.

She was telling us this guy wouldn't make it to date number two; not because the cat peed on her stuff but because the guy in fact owned a cat. "I'm sorry" she said, "but do you know of any guys that have cats as their pet of choice?" "Umm, well what about Glenn?" our one friend Liv asked. "That's different", Gwen said! "Glenn only had Mr. Whiskers because it was his and Jackie's cat and when she left him, her new landlord wouldn't allow cats, so he got stuck with the little fluff ball." "Ok, ok makes sense then" Liv said. "Nope still weird". Lizzie said. "He can cuddle his cat at night, because it won't be with me!" We all laughed and decided to lift our glasses and cheers goodbye to the "cat guy."

My phone started ringing from my purse then. I remember it shocked me because my phone was always set on silent but I had an important job interview I was waiting to hear back from so I had turned the ringer on that day. "Sorry guys; I have to be that person and check my phone quick!" I looked at the number calling me and felt like someone instantly punched my gut which jumped up to my throat and then back down to my gut.

"What's wrong?" Gwen asked. I couldn't even speak; all I could do was turn the phone towards them and mouth oh my god! It was Josh Wilson calling me. Josh Wilson! Josh, my ex-boyfriend who I hadn't heard from or seen in two plus years. Josh, who I thought was going to be my future husband but instead turned into a future ex. How is it that someone you don't see or hear from for that long can still give you that kind of reaction as if you just saw them yesterday? I watched as each of my friends jaws collectively opened as wide as mine did. "Maybe he dialed the wrong number," I said suddenly, trying to convince myself. "Like maybe there's two Elle's in his phone and he meant to call the other one". "Uh yeah, yeah that's probably it" the girls' words swirled together. I noticed one of them was inching my glass closer to me and I was about to put it up to my mouth when my phone did the text ring. I looked down at the phone, while all of us did the same. We all sat in silence for a moment until I then picked it up. When I looked at it, I saw a text had popped up from Josh.

"Hey you! Long time no talk. Gimme a call. I miss you Ellie" ;) Hey you, that was always what he would say to me when he saw me. Plus, Ellie ... no one but him called me that. No doubt about it; this was meant for me alright. I miss you? He missed me? How could he miss me? Especially after all of this time? I threw my phone out to the middle of the table while Liv snatched it up first as if it was a wedding bouquet that had hit the floor. She gasped and shook her head and I watched them each read the text and react in the same way. I felt myself break out into a cold sweat and everything in me tensed up. I knew I needed to get the hell out of dodge immediately. "Ummm ... air. I need to... I think I'm going to be... yeah I need air", was all I was able to get out. Liv and Gwen stood up looking concerned and I put my hands out and said "No! No! Umm just order some strong shots I'll be right back. I just need to be alone for a moment."

I shot up from my chair and of course it had to make the loudest sound as the leg of the chair scraped against the wooden floor. Is everyone staring at me or did I become suddenly paranoid? Eh whatever; I need to find the exit right now. I start to pick up my pace as I make the longest exit in history and finally the door is opened and I can take a moment and breathe in the air. Air away from my phone, air away from Josh. I can feel my heart beating out of my chest; like maybe I should be concerned. Can a twenty-five-year-old have a heart attack? I can see the headlines on the article written about my demise already. Twenty-five-year-old dies from ex-boyfriend texting her. Read all about her desperate life. I don't even realize that I'm breathing heavily and leaning against the cold windows at the side of the restaurant until I see one of the chefs looking straight at me saying something.

"Huh?" That's all I can say because I know he's talking but I can't hear words. "Are you ok?" He asks with concern. Ok, my focus is starting to come in clearer now. I turn around and see my hand is up against the brick wall. How did I even get to the side of the building? I must've been pressed up along the side like I'm scaling a skyscraper. Get a hold of yourself Elle, I tell myself. I can see behind this mystery guy a few other employees sitting on those old crates they use for produce and packaged food as their chairs and they're smoking cigarettes. "Can I have a cigarette?" I ask suddenly. "A cigarette? Miss, I don't know if you should; you don't even seem to be breathing normally let alone having smoke get in and mix in with all of that" the man says. "Look, with all due respect, if I wanted your expert opinion, I'd go to a doctor not a cook so please can I have a cigarette?"

"Ok, ok hang on, geez" he says with a side smile and I notice his fingers are shaking a little as he pulls a cigarette out for me and grabs a lighter. I haven't had a cigarette in years but I figure now is as good a time as any. I place the cigarette in my mouth as he puts one hand on the lighter and uses the other to block the wind from letting the fire burn out. I take a big inhale and start coughing immediately. "Yeah, see; I figured this would happen" he says as he smiles. "You'll be ok, cheer up sweet pea." "Don't tell me to cheer up and don't call me sweet pea" I yell in between puffs. "Whoa, you're a little prickly one, aren't you?" he says as he puts his hands up in defense holding the cigarette in his mouth. "Ok, so … prickly like a pear. How about cheer up sweet pear?"

There's a moment of silence as I pause and then the weirdest thing happens. I start laughing. Like full on body shaking laughing where you can't tell if someone is crying or laughing because they sound like a crazy hyena. He starts laughing too because the thing with someone laughing like that is it's contagious. "That doesn't even make sense" I say in between laughs while holding my side. "Pears aren't prickly, what kind of chef are you?" "Well technically they're in the cactus family" he says, "but anyway, if it's getting you laughing then it doesn't matter." I realize then that he didn't mean the pear fruit I was thinking of and this makes me laugh even more. When I finally get control of myself, I say, "thank you; I needed that. I'm sorry…this is like a typical girl scenario. Ex-boyfriend who tormented ex- girlfriend calls her years later, tells her he misses her and girl goes into a full-on meltdown." "Well, with all due respect sweet pear" he says; "Don't shoot the messenger but this guy sounds like a jerk and there's nothing about you that seems like a typical girl. Take that as a compliment."

I'm left speechless. No one has ever said anything that romantic to me. I look up at him slowly and it's like I'm looking at this man for the first time. It's then I notice too that he's been crouching next to me this whole time so that he can stand at my height. He has beautiful, soulful, warm blue eyes and when he smiles, he has this little dimple that appears. Who is this guy? As if he has read my mind, he puts his hand out and says, "My name is Ryan by the way. Ryan Elverson." "Hi", I say as I place a piece of my blonde hair behind my ear. "My name's Elle. Elle Green."

Chapter Four

Out of my daydream, I'm aware again that I'm driving. It's crazy to me how your mind can go onto autopilot while driving. It's been years since I've driven to this house but it's like I could find my way here with my eyes closed. I'm now turning on the road where Josh lives, and now I do too, I guess? I really hope he's not home, please don't be home, please don't be home I recite to myself. Well, that's a change of pace; I remember when we were dating and living together, I used to pray the opposite. Josh was never home; always out with his buddies or out at the bar where he said he was making extra tip money but ironically, he was never able to pay bills on time, or sometimes at all. Alright; think about what Gwen said, I think to myself. I have to act like I'm happily married or he will know something's up. I have to take all of this resentment and push it aside.

That's the thing I realize. I never got closure from this guy. So maybe I can get it here? Maybe this is some test or something where if I get the closure I need, I can get back to my old life, with Ryan. I'm pulling up to the house now and I don't see any cars in the driveway. Ok thank God, I think. I can have some time to myself to investigate a little bit.

After trying out three different keys on my keyring, I finally find the one that lets me inside. Yes, this is Josh's house but it's also very different. It actually has a cozy vibe if I'm being completely honest. Not at all the same place I remember that reeked of bachelorhood as much as I tried to change it. Now though, now I can see the feminine touch has made its way through. There are several throw pillows on the couch and a fleece blanket draped over the side. That's so me, I think. Ok, at least I'm still myself here. I still have my sense of style and identity. I also notice how there are several candles sprinkled throughout the living room, dining room and kitchen. Then, it basically hits me in the face. Our wedding photo on the wall. This thing is huge; like obnoxiously huge. It sits on the wall above the fireplace and it's in black and white. Hmm ... is that a metaphor of our marriage? Our life is missing that vibrancy; that color that shows that we're alive and happy? I get up close to it to inspect our faces. I look genuinely happy; like I can't take my hands off of him, but that's how I always was with Josh. I was always drawn to him like Cupid came around, hit me with an arrow and skipped away like, Man that was easy!

Just as I remember meeting Ryan for the first time; I also remember meeting Josh. I was a little over twenty-one years old and still felt new at the whole drinking in public thing. It was my college roommate's birthday and she wanted to have a night she didn't remember. We were on our third bar stop that was on the same street and had two more to go but I had a feeling she wouldn't make it. She was fighting with her boyfriend the whole time because he was supposed to be joining us and he couldn't until later. When he finally walked through the door with an air of confidence, she was ready to fight. He ordered our drinks and before they even took their first sips, she started accusing him of cheating, left the bar and he followed her out. I looked at my Cosmopolitan and thought ok...well, it's already paid for so I might as well drink it.

The bartender came up to me then. I felt his presence before actually seeing his face. When I looked at him, we locked eyes and my God, it was instant. I have never been more aware of my sexuality as I had in that first moment of looking into his eyes. What is in this drink? I thought. I immediately felt my cheeks blush and the warmth radiate downwards as I was imagining all of the things I wanted to do to this stranger. Then he spoke. "Tough break", he acknowledged as the corner of his mouth upturned which showed off a dimple on each side. What can I say, I've always been a sucker for dimples!

"So, are your friends coming back or did they leave you alone?" He asked. His voice sounded like the perfect mixture of velvet and honey. It was as if his mere presence was fulfilling every one of my senses that I didn't know I wanted or needed to be filled. "Umm", I nervously said. "Yeah, I don't know. They do this sometimes, and they usually don't come back." "What, leave you with their unattended drinks, because that's pretty cool actually." "Yeah, I never thought about it like that," I said. "I guess I could drink them, unless that would be frowned upon by the bartender?" Was I flirting? I don't even know what I was saying but I was hoping my words were making some kind of sense. "Frowned upon?" He asked. "Nah, it'll be our little secret. I won't tell if you don't tell I'm doing this," he said with a little laugh as he showed me he was pouring vodka into his glass of soda he had under the bar. "I saw nothing!" I giggled. "Yeah, well that's funny, because I'm sure seeing something", he said as he looked me up and down in a way that literally took my breath away.

I'll admit as I'm remembering this very story, I'm starting to feel warm. It's crazy how when I revisit memories it almost feels as if I'm back in that moment again. My heart starts to beat, my palms get sweaty and I can literally hear my breathing getting labored. As if on cue on a script, I hear the door open. What does he sniff out pheromones? I think. Ok I've got to look normal, what do I do with myself? I decide to grab my phone and sit at the barstools surrounding our island in the kitchen.

"Hello again Ellie," he says, looking at me side-eyed and laughs as he puts down the bags he's holding. "Again?" I ask. Wait, is this happening to him too? "What do you mean again?" I repeat. "This morning", he says. "When you said nice to see you? Sheesh, what's up with you? Sounds like someone's doing too many meditations recently, you're losing touch with reality." Hmmm, good idea Josh, I think. I'll do a meditation later and see if anything comes up. Maybe I'll get some insight into what's going on

"Oh, haha yeah," I laugh. "Just keeping you on your toes." "Well anyway", he says, "I picked up sandwiches from Lorenzo's. I got to go but I'll see you later." "Oh, where are you going?" I ask. "Uhhh out" he replies quickly. Of course, I think. He hasn't changed a bit. "Oh ok", I say as I look down, feeling a semblance of loneliness. "Just kidding", he laughs as he taps me on the shoulder. "I know how much you hate that. I'm going to the driving range with Jim but I'll be back in time for dinner." He then comes up behind me, swivels the bar chair around and lifts me out of the chair with my legs wrapped around his waist. "Unless you give me a reason to stay," he whispers. Oh my God I think; he's still so good at the seduction game. No no no, I think...snap out of it. "Oh, yeah that'd be nice but you go! I'll see you at dinner", I say as I turn my head to the side and look down.

He looks confused for a minute and then plops me back down on the chair. "Uh, yeah ok. Alright Ellie, later!" He grabs his sandwich out of the bag and is back out of the house just as quickly as he walked in.

What the hell was that? I think. How does he get me all hot and bothered so quickly and after all of this time? This was different though. His reaction. Something tells me Ellie doesn't say no to Josh often.

Chapter Five

I take a shower in my unfamiliar yet somewhat familiar home and sit down on the plush white couch. I could never have any white furniture with Ryan because he would come home from the restaurant and plop right down still in his work clothes which would then in turn have a trail of crumbs or grease stains left behind. I spent the last hour scavenging my house looking for clues. I've found nothing. Nothing! Not a single journal, letter, scribble on a piece of paper that says "HELP" in capital letters, nothing. Want to hear the real kicker? My phone did a mysterious update while I was at Gwen's and shocker, all texts are wiped clean. I mean seriously; what kind of Twilight Zone episode is this? The only call on my log is the one I made to Josh before. I don't understand; I mean it's one thing to completely forget a marriage, but another to also remember a completely different one with a different guy!

I wish I had Ryan's number so I could call him and see if he remembers me, that I'm not in fact crazy. I have to remember what Gwen told me. Play the part right now Elle! See what this is all about and don't do anything rash. Ok, ok I can at least take the night in and see what life with Josh is like. It's so ironic, when we were dating all I wanted was to marry him. Especially when we broke up, I clung to all of our conversations about what our wedding would look like, how many kids we'd have, the whole nine yards. Yet now here I am, "married" to Josh and all I want to do is run.

    I decide to have a glass of wine to calm me down. I mean it is five o'clock now so it's acceptable, right? Oh, and also coupled with the fact I technically already drank at ten AM. God; that feels like a lifetime ago. Maybe time works differently now? Ugh so many thoughts, too many thoughts; time to have a glass and unwind. I open the fridge and am disappointed to see no wine chilling. All that's in this fridge seems to be craft beers. Geez, I don't even have my own identity with my food, I think to myself. When I've finally found the wine rack, which by the way is downstairs in the basement; I pick the one that seems to be the most expensive Cabernet and bring it back upstairs with me.

    The sound of the cork popping and my wine pouring into my empty glass makes me feel like home again. So maybe, home is where the wine is? I sit down on the couch and turn on the TV to see what I have recorded on the DVR. Looks like a whole season of the Bachelor. Hmm it's Juan Pablo's season. That's interesting because that's an old season that I've never watched. I guess I'll start now.

    Two episodes in and I start to get hungry. I check my phone, no calls or messages from Josh. He did say he'd be back for dinner but it's seven now and no sign of him in sight. I send him a text because it seems like the right thing to do when your husband hasn't returned. "Hey Josh!" erase erase..."hey babe" ... erase babe that feels weird... "hey! I'm gonna order Chinese, do you want anything? I know you said you'd be back for dinner so...just checking." At 7:10, I check my phone once. At 7:20, I've turned the screen on and off 3 times and I realize it's brought me back to a time I've experienced before.

    We had been dating for about six months and he told me he was going to the bar. "On your day off", I had asked. "Yeah, the guys want to have a drink and I can actually drink with them instead of watching them drink so I'm gonna take them up on it." "Oh, ok" I said, feeling left out. "Can I come or meet up with you all later? I like your friends." "Ehh", he paused. "Yeah, I don't know," he said while he ran his fingers through his hair. "It's kind of a guy's night, but you'll be fine, have a great night", he said as he gave me a quick kiss on the cheek. I leaned in, wanting more. Always wanting more from him. "What time will you be back?" I yelled as he was rushing past me to the door. "No later than eleven!" he had said without looking back at me.

Well, that didn't happen. It was 11:30 and I remember thinking to myself ok, maybe he hit traffic. I sent a text. No response back. Midnight, no response. 1 AM, I had called his phone on repeat, ten times my phone had shown me. 2 AM, I had called twenty times and now it was going straight to voicemail. I tried to sleep but couldn't bring myself to sleep in our bed. It felt wrong without him; like the bed wasn't fully mine. It was ours. I uncomfortably shifted side to side on the scratchy couch while trying not to make eye contact with my clock that showed me it was 3 AM. By 4 AM, I was sitting up sobbing thinking he got into an accident. I had texted his friends, called him thirty times and sent so many text messages it looked like I was stalking him. Finally, at 5 AM, he came home. He gave me some kind of excuse about going out with the guys and his phone dying and he passed out on Jake's couch. Then, he had the nerve to try to have sex with me! Here's where the shameful part comes in that I've never told any of my friends, I let him.

Chapter Six

I pop out of my past thought bubble and am back in present time on my white couch with my glass of Cabernet almost spilling onto the furniture.

I wipe away tears that had begun to roll down my cheeks while I was in deep thought of this past moment as well. "Wow", I say out loud. "Man, Elle, you put up with so much from this jerk. Why did you continue and marry him? I know there were happy moments too in our relationship but I can't think about that right now. Alright, well, past Elle would have kept calling him and calling him but not present Elle. Present Elle is ordering Chinese, for herself only."

At 8:00, not only does my food arrive but it's also around when Josh calls me. "Ellie" he slurs as I answer the phone. "Hi baby, I just saw your text. I'm sorry." "Hey", I say with no emotion in my tone. "No prob, the food was just delivered but since I didn't hear back, I didn't get you anything so hope you're eating!" "Oh", he says followed by a little pause. "Uh yeah that's fine. Maybe save me some of yours because I am really hungry, got to feed this growing boy." I look around at my containers filled with low mein, white rice, crab rangoons, and pint of wonton soup and say "Yeah sorry; I only got enough for me." "You're mad", he says with a laugh. "No, I'm not",

I say. "I'm used to this Josh and I'm tired so I'm going to eat my dinner and see you when I see you." "Alright" he says awkwardly. "Well, I'm heading home soon. I just wanted to put in my order but it's ok I'll figure something else out. See you in a little while baby. I love you, my Ellie!" "Alright buh bye", I say and hang up. I throw my phone to the other couch cushion with one hand while I lick off the red sauce from my Chinese that has formed on the side of my glass. I know, I'm surprised my husband isn't rushing home to see me too!

I continue watching The Bachelor and am seeing how the girls are saying it's hard for them to watch Juan Pablo kiss all these girls in front of them. I remember I used to think, well you know what you signed up for so why are you surprised? Now, though, my thoughts have changed. Now I look at it how even though you know or you think you know what you're signing up for, it all changes when you develop feelings. I mean yeah, it would be hard if I was there for Ryan's heart and I saw him kissing other girls right after kissing me. How can they do that? I couldn't imagine kissing so many guys one after the other and as I think this, something happens. It's like a quick jerking motion and I watch as I drop my crab rangoon which plops into the sweet and sour sauce which then splatters all over the white couch.

"Dammit" I yell out loud. Hmm maybe this is why Ryan didn't want to get white furniture. Here I am blaming it on him when, if I'm being honest, it would be awful for me as well because I'm a super klutz, especially when I'm eating.

After looking up how to clean stains from white furniture I finally am able to get it out. I get into my pajamas, climb into bed and feel like I can finally get my mind to stop swirling when I hear the front door creak open.

This time I don't look at my phone because I don't care what the time is. I hear Josh brush his teeth, flush the toilet and then walk into the bedroom and strip down to his boxers. He slinks into bed next to me and I feel him drape his arm over my waist. "Hi baby", he whispers in my ear. I can smell the stale beer he's been drinking on his breath and try not to cough as I'm pretending to be asleep. "Ellie?" he asks and shakes me a little. "You awake babe? Don't be mad at me, I'm sorry. I'll make it up to you tomorrow, or right now if you want?" Stay still, I think. Do not move or make a sound. Of course, I have the most insane itch on my face that I am certain is a restraint test. Mind over matter, I think. Mind over matter. "Ellie?" He asks again. "Ugh fine", he says under his breath. "Guess I won't make it up to you after all." He turns over angrily and grabs the blankets with a quick tug. I get the biggest, Grinchiest grin on my face. Night one with Josh was a bust, and further proves to me how I need to figure out what's going on and how to get out of this mixed-up life.

Chapter Seven

I have a confession I need to tell you all about. No, I did not sleep with Josh! I did remember something though. It happened when I was thinking about the Bachelor and kissing one person after the other. It was like I had a flashback but it was part of the puzzle I couldn't figure out yesterday morning. When I remembered it, it actually jolted me which is why I dropped the crab rangoon which you know led to what I'm pretty sure is still showing remnants on the couch, no matter how hard I scrubbed.

Ok, so the confession part. This is going to be hard to hear and I hope it doesn't change your opinion of me. I don't know yet why it happened but the point is it happened.

As I remembered earlier, I had been at a martini bar with my girlfriends, married to Ryan. I'm certain of that. We had car service set up, no one was driving so we were 4 women ready to let loose. We each went around the circle basically having a good bitch session about things our husbands and boyfriends do that drive us crazy and after each one would share, we would lift our martini glasses and say, cheers that we've got each other! This went on for a little bit and I was in the middle of saying, "Ryan drives me nuts when he gets those little hairs all over the bathroom sink after shaving, like how is it even, oh my God!" "What's wrong?" Lizzie asks quickly. Gwen is the first to follow my stare and see it ends right at Josh Wilson whom we all haven't seen in years.

It's like the music literally stops as blood drains from my body and then is syringed back in and pulsing. I try to recover but I've made my reaction known to my friends and it seems I've sent a telepathic message over to Josh because right before I go to look away, his eyes are on me.

We stare for what feels like minutes but it's probably only five seconds and he does a little wave as he starts walking towards us. Gwen says low, "he's coming, he's coming." "I know, shut up Gwen!", I say. "Act cool, act cool. Sorry didn't mean to tell you to shut up"; I stammer out in a run-on sentence. "No, it's fine", she says. "I get it, not acting cool though" she mentions and I laugh a genuine, half nervous laugh as I hear "Ellie Green? Wow you are the last person I expected to see tonight." "Hey Josh", I say, sounding as confident as I can make myself sound. "Yeah, you too." "It's Elverson", Gwen says quickly and with emphasis. "What?" he asks. "Her name is Elle Elverson."

"Oh, you got married?" he asks. "I did", I say with the biggest smile as I watch the disappointment spread across his face. Oh, this feels good, I think. Yeah, now he can see how I dodged a huge bullet by not being with him. Although, I'd be lying if I said he didn't look good. He does, really good. I know better though, but there's no harm in being polite.

He starts to tell me about his life, how he's working on developing his own whiskey and the girls start to talk amongst themselves as a.) The conversation is boring to them and b.) It's weird with us just talking and them sitting there looking like deer in headlights. I thank my lucky stars I have on the outfit I have on. It's an oversized but also curve-hugging gray sweater dress along with thigh high black suede boots. I know I look hot and I know he thinks I look hot. One of the biggest perks but also the curse of knowing someone on an intimate level is what their signals are when they're turned on.

Josh's are easy. He makes eye contact with me but every so often scans where my boot begins to where it ends. He also will be in mid-sentence and lose his train of thought followed by a quick, "I'm sorry, I forgot what I was saying." "Well, the whiskey thing sounds cool," I say. "It was nice to see you." I could've kept the conversation going but I know I need to cut it short. "You too", he says. "Can I give you a hug? Sorry, if that's weird." "No, it's fine", I say and as I stand up, I can hear one of the girls gasp and say "oh my god" under their breath. I can faintly hear one of them ordering us another round of drinks. My girls know me so well.

Anyway, we hug and it does feel familiar. He smells the same to me, but I make sure to pull away first. As I'm pulling away, he whispers in my ear, "your husband's a very lucky guy." Time stands still for a moment. Here's the thing; you can tell your mind to stop it but your body is a force on its own. As he says these words, my body breaks out into goosebumps. Shoot, this is my signal. Thank God this sweater covers my arms. "He is", I smile as I say goodbye and sit back down.

The girls know to give it a full ten seconds of silence before saying "So, what the hell was that?" "What?" I ask. I was acting mature, grown up, polite. "He doesn't deserve politeness," Gwen says. He's like an avocado. "What?" Liv asks with confusion. "Please explain."

"Well,", Gwen says as she licks the salt off of her margarita glass (looks like we've moved onto margs). "Avocados can show such promise. It can feel right on the outside but there's nothing worse when you slice them open and they're all rotten inside. He's like that! Yeah, he looks cute and you can still cut your sexual tension with a knife but inside, dudes no good. For you or any female for that matter."

"Sexual tension?" I ask, trying to keep a sly smile from forming. "No, maybe once, but not anymore." "Oh yeah?" Lizzie asks. "Then why did your cheeks all of a sudden look flushed?" Dammit, I think. Turns out not only your exes can spot your signals.

Chapter Eight

You know when you're aware someone's looking at you but you can't dare look to see? You can literally feel their laser eyes on your back. Well, I've been playing that game with Josh for about a half hour after he left our table. The girls told me he was there with some other guys; I'm sure I may even know them but I don't care to find out. We are on our second round of margaritas when a tray of shots is brought to our table. "What is this?" Liv asks. "Tequila shots," the waitress tells us. "They're from the guy over there at the bar." Guess who? Yeah, Josh is giving us a wave. "Oh my God, this guy won't quit!" Lizzie says. "Maybe he's just being nice?" Liv tries to reason. "No", Gwen jumps in; "he's not. He's being calculated but I'm not going to turn down a free shot so pass me the limes please. To us", Gwen says as she lifts her shot up. "To us", we all repeat and as I take the shot, I feel my phone vibrate. The next few minutes go by pretty quickly so instead of going back and forth I'll show you how the texts went below.

Josh- Is this still your number Ellie?

Josh- It must be, because I just saw you look at your phone. Unless your husband messaged you at the same time which is strange if that happened.

I take my phone and put it back in my clutch. Nope, not gonna play this game. Shoot, he just saw me look at him. Dammit! I feel another vibration.

Josh- Caught you! ;)

I feel my face turn hot again. Damn this guy, I think. Ok fine, I'll just text thank you for the shots. Cut it short but also be polite and "above it".

Me- Knock it off. Thank you for the shots, you didn't need to do that.

Josh- I know I didn't need to but I wanted to. I really hope this isn't out of line to say but I forgot how beautiful you are.

Me- You forgot? Uhm thanks? Way to give me a backhanded compliment Wilson.

Josh- It was supposed to be a compliment. I guess you make me nervous, Green.

Me- It's Elverson.

Gwen- What are you doing?

Gwen? Crap! I look up and see her give me a look that speaks volumes. So, I text her back.

Me 2 Gwen- What?

Gwen- Don't try to play me girl, I know who you're talking to. What is he saying?

Me 2 Gwen- How do you do that? It's creepy actually how well you know me. Anyway... he's not saying anything really, it's harmless honestly. Also, I kind of like having the power, playing with fire won't hurt anyone.

Gwen- Mm hmm... until you wait too long to blow the candle out and you get burned.

Josh- That's right. Yeah, I like Green better. How weird though that after all this time we run into each other? Sorry if I overstepped. I just wanted you to know how beautiful you still very much are.

Me- Well, thank you I appreciate it. Have a good night.

Josh- You too Ellie.

Me 2 Gwen- It's done. I ended the convo, happy?

Gwen- Are you?

 I put my phone back in my clutch then and nod my head to Gwen that yes, I am happy. Deep down I am and she knows that. Ryan and I have just been in a rough patch for the past year, or two. It happens in marriage. Especially when your husband is trying to start his own business and own his own restaurant. There are late nights and sometimes I'll admit; I feel single. Sometimes I miss the harmless flirting, which is exactly what this is.

 A few hours later it's me, Gwen and Liv left as Lizzie had to dodge out early. We are at that point in the night where we slur a little but don't dare call each other out on it. I've been holding in having to pee for the past hour but haven't made the move yet. I don't know why but I get in these moods where I go on a stubborn strike with my body and refuse myself to get up and go. Also, I hate breaking the seal. It's a real thing, by the way. Although I've tried my hardest, I can't take it anymore so I stand up. Oh, ok. Yeah, I'm drunk, I think as I wobble a little into my chair. How is it when you stand up it's like suddenly a neon signal is sent to your brain that says guess what, this girl is sloshed!

 There's a line of girls waiting for the bathroom. "Oh my God really?!" I cry out with frustration. The tall girl standing in front of me turns around and says, "Yeah apparently they only have one toilet in each bathroom, like why?" "That makes no sense," I say. "I know," she smiles back. "I love your boots by the way!" "Thank you", I smile. "I love your hair!" She has her hair in those fishtail braid pigtails that only someone with perfect volumized hair can pull off. It's at this point I'm doing a full-on pee sway move right now feeling like my bladder is going to burst when Josh comes out of the guy's bathroom.

"Oh, here we go!" I say dramatically. "What?" he laughs. "Are you following me?" I ask. "Look", he says as he steps closer to me. "Clearly I was in the bathroom first so if anyone is following anyone it's you following me!" He notices then that I've been almost completely turning my torso back and forth. "You gonna be ok?" he asks me. "No, my bladder is gonna collapse!" I say "And of course the girl's bathroom always has a line!" "Use the dudes," he says. "Gross, I don't even wanna know what it's like in there." "Well, that's rude," he says. "And, I'll have you know it actually smells pretty nice in there, I think they have like a lilac plug in or something." I giggle a little and realize I miss our banter. "Married Elle, married to Ryan. Cut it off now Elle. It's just harmless flirting" is what my mind is telling me as I wrestle with back-and-forth emotions.

"Well, I can't go in there because that's not fair to the other women waiting in line", I say. "No girl you do you", the girl with nice hair turns around and says to me. "Yeah girl", Josh says. "You do you." This makes me laugh and I say, "Alright fine, but if someone comes in, I'm gonna flip out!" "I'll stand guard," Josh offers. "No, no I can take care of myself" I slur as I tap his chest with my hand. "You just turn yourself around and walk back to your whiskey drinking friends and go ahead and buy some other girls some shots." "Yeah, so I'm definitely gonna keep guard", he says then. "I don't trust other guys around you right now."

I would argue more but I'm definitely going to pee myself so I go in and close the door. As I'm washing my hands, I look at myself in the mirror and say quietly, "You pull yourself together Elle. Do not act drunk! You are fine, you are beautiful and you are strong. Yeah, I'm drunk" I say. Just to make it even more known to myself my level of intoxication I proceed to wink at myself in the mirror before exiting. I open the door and it catches weirdly. The heel of my boot pushes back and I trip over myself as Josh catches me before I fall.

"Well, that just happened!" I say loudly with dramatic effect. "You ok Elle?" he asks me and I see in his eyes he actually really looks concerned. "I'm fine Josh really. The door caught and my heel did something weird and, thank you for catching me", I say as I'm trying to fix my wild hair that blew in front of my face. Next thing I know Josh is slowly placing a piece of my hair behind my ear and looking at me strangely. "Why are you looking at me like that?" I ask. "Like what?" he softly chokes out with a hint of surprise and a dash of arousal. "You're looking at me like you want to devour me." I can't believe I just said that but I did. "Well," he says as he clears his throat. "Devour is a big word but Jesus Ellie, after all of this time, you still are so freaking irresistible to me. I'm sorry but I can't help myself", he says.

He takes a step closer and now has both hands on each side of the wall behind me pinning me against it. My brain is literally playing a game of tug of war with the words no and yes. I miss feeling this way; miss being talked to like this, looked at this way. I catch a whiff of his scent and I know I'm probably going to let this happen. It's too much; I just can't stop the force that's coming out from inside of me. He pauses right as he's about an inch away from my mouth and says, "God, I want you, Ellie." Then I do it. My hand grasps a fistful of his hair behind his head and I use that momentum to bring him to me. Our lips meet and I'm the one devouring him. My hand then moves from his head down to his muscular back and I pull him closer as his pelvis is now grinding right up against me. His hands have moved from the wall to around my butt as he squeezes me which has slowly made my dress ride up. I'm completely lost in the moment of lust and passion. It's like I've left my body and I'm now in the corner watching this happen to someone else. I'm cheering for this girl to give into her feral desire not caring or thinking that she has a husband at home.

I have a husband at home. "Ryan!" I yell out as I pull back suddenly. "What?" Josh asks with confusion as I see the blacks of his pupils are as big as someone rolling on ecstasy and his lips are smeared red from my lipstick. "Holy screwup" I mutter out as I put my hand to the scene of the crime, my mouth. "I can't. Nope. Nope. I'm sorry Josh. No, I, I have to go!" I basically run away, go to the table, grab my clutch and say, "I'll send you guys what I owe you,

I'm not feeling well," all in one swift motion without making eye contact. Gwen stands up and follows me out and I know she knows. I feel sick and I go to the side of the building outside and do in fact throw up.

Chapter Nine

I'm a terrible person, I know. It's ok; take a moment to call me whatever you want, I can take it. I'm washing my face the next morning looking at myself in the mirror. So, it seems the Bachelor helped me recall this terrible thing I must have hidden in the depths of my brain. If that's the case, are there other things lurking in there? How could I have done this? I cheated on my husband, I deserve all of this now, I think. I call Gwen and ask her to meet me at the park nearby so I can fill her in on my discovery.

I finish telling her everything and get to the part where I throw up and she is just looking at me. "What?" I ask. "You hate me, I'm a terrible person," I say. "Go ahead, say it, what are you thinking?"

"Well," she finally says. "Did I at least hold your hair while you threw up? Cause if I didn't then I'm the crappy friend, not you." I give her a huge hug and say, "God, I love you!" "I love you too," she said, and "look, this happened for a reason. Do I agree with what you did? No, mostly because I hate Josh but you're human Elle and it sounds like you were going through a very fragile time in your marriage with Ryan. When someone is in a vulnerable state, they're susceptible to do things they know are wrong but do it because it feels good. I can't judge you for that. You obviously feel remorse. So, time to cut yourself some slack and figure out your next move."

"Wait, you hate Josh?" I interrupt. "I mean before you alluded to something but said you'd keep your opinions to yourself. What do you know that I don't know?" "Shoot", she says. "Well, I lasted a day, right? Not bad. How do I explain", she says as she takes a pause. "I don't like who you are around him. You shrivel up, you're on edge and he dims your light. Do I think he loves you? I do but I think if you took the physical part out of the relationship, you'd be able to see more clearly. I also think he knows that and plays to that."

"Ok", I say. "This is all good information. He actually tried to sleep with me yesterday, twice and I said no." "Wow", she says, "I bet that threw him for a loop. That's like a record from what you tell me."

Hmmm that's useful information that I take and file in my brain. He's not used to me saying no to him. I still struggle with how this actually happened as I try to make sense of it. "So ok", I say as I think out loud. "I kissed him, while married to Ryan. Why though, would that bring me to being married to Josh? Like did that do something that brought me to a different track in life? Like a right turn at the fork in the road? I made my decision by marrying Ryan and cutting off communication altogether with Josh so how could one moment, one kiss change the whole trajectory?" "That, I do not know", Gwen says. "I still think you have a lesson or something to learn with Josh so keep playing house and see what comes out of it."

Chapter Ten

I'm on my way back home and decide to take a different road and somehow end up pulling up next to where Sweet Pear is located. Alright, I'll admit it, I drove here on purpose. I just wanted to see if I could catch a glimpse of Ryan and what his dream coming to life looks like. Well damn, it does not disappoint. It's so cute, like modern day chic meets southern belle. It's probably for the best that the restaurant isn't open yet because I know I'd be tempted to go in. I do spot a coffee shop down the road though so I decide to stop in for a quick latte.

When I walk in, the door has one of those jingle bell things attached to it which makes everyone in line turn around and look at me. "Hi", I say out loud to everyone as I do a dramatic swipe across wave. Gosh, I can be so awkward sometimes. I'm scanning the inside of the coffee shop and it literally looks like one of those places you see in Hallmark Christmas movies. The tables are wooden but rustic looking and have holly covered tablecloths on them. They even have a chalkboard menu that has a countdown until Christmas on it. It's cute but I mean it's early November and I'm not in the best headspace for Christmas merry and cheer right now.

The barista, who by the way is wearing an apron that says, "Santa visits here a latte" asks me what I'd like. I'm sure she's pleased when I tell her I definitely want a latte but I'm deciding between the apple cinnamon muffin and the chocolate croissant. "Eh I'll get both please", I decide. She tells me the amount I owe which is $10.24 and I'm digging in my wallet and only find a ten-dollar bill. "Shoot", I say with embarrassment. "Umm, this was an impulse trip so I didn't bring my card with me and only have ten dollars. Can I run to my car quickly and see if I can find the change?" Before she can answer, there's a male voice behind me saying, "It's ok Kelly, I'll cover this lady's amount." I would recognize that voice anywhere and so does my heart as it literally feels like it's skipping. It's Ryan.

I turn around and there he is. If he were a bottled-up scent, he'd be called *Mountain Springs* because he just makes me feel like I can breathe clean air again and feel at peace. His brown hair is perfectly tousled and he has a little bit of scruff on his face that I have to admit I like. He's wearing a long black peacoat with a red scarf tied around him and, gosh he just looks so handsome. "Hiii", I say with way too much excitement. "Hello," he says back very professionally. It kind of throws me for a loop, I don't know what I was expecting. Did I think he'd see me and the spell would be lifted? I know what I must look like right now, I'm staring at him so I have to make small talk in a non-creepy way. "Do I know you", I ask. What the hell Elle? That was terrible. Try again, I tell myself. "I mean, you look familiar, are you a chef?" That wasn't really that much better but it's too late now.

He smiles and there's that sweet dimple forming on his cheek. "I am actually," he says. "Right down the street, Sweet Pear." "Oh, I love that place!" I say. Kelly, the barista gives me my items and I stall at the napkin station so that I can have more time to talk to Ryan. "Yeah?" he says, "Well thank you. It's always nice to meet a loyal customer. I hope you have a great day Miss." "Elle!" I say, a little too fast. "My name is Elle. Thank you for paying the rest of my order too; you didn't have to do that." "You're welcome, Elle", he says back. "My name's Ryan. It was nice to meet you", he says as he takes a sip of his coffee and turns towards the door.

He's leaving and I have to keep him here a little longer. I'm not ready to be separated from his energy yet! Before I can censor myself, I shout out after him, "Wait, I have a question." He turns around with a confused look on his face that he's able to recover quickly. "I have an answer, go ahead," he says with an intriguing side smile. "Umm, I have to ask. Where did you get the name for your restaurant? I mean it's so unique." "Oh", he chuckles. "Yeah, that's a very special nickname to me." "Oh?" I prod. I wonder if he's given it to someone else and my heart sinks. If there's another woman that he has claimed with this name I'll shrivel up and die. "Yeah, you see, my grandfather gave that nickname to my grandma when they first met and he still calls her by it. They're the greatest love story I've really ever known so it seemed fitting. Anyway, I have to go but maybe I'll see you in there soon. Take care Elle", he says and like that he's gone and I'm left watching this man walk away in awe. My husband is so beautiful, I think. What in the world have I done?

    I decide to sit down with my latte and baked goods to collect myself. He seems so different. His whole vibe has changed, in a good way. Is it because he doesn't know me right now and I get to see the side of him everyone else does? No because he's never been a different person to others than he was to me, except when he's stressed. That happens to anyone though, right? Stress brings out the worst of people.

    The thing that's really hard for me to wrap my brain around is that I was just an encounter right now. A passing person on the street. I don't know what I was expecting. Did I think he'd fall in love with me instantly? Did I think I'd have the same effect on him as I did when we first met? My heart hurts a little and I know I have to change my thought process. Whatever this is, this is meant to happen for some reason. If I'm meant to run into him again, I will. If I don't ... well I can't think about that right now. I need to focus on why I'm in the relationship I'm in currently is happening.

    So many things confuse me about why I'm married to Josh. Did I settle? How did he end up committing? The way we had left things definitely didn't add up to this.

Another thing that bothers me is that Gwen told me I'm a stay-at-home wife and that I haven't written in ages. Huh? Why would I stop doing that? I love to write. Writing had become my identity, so who was I without it? When I asked her why I stopped she said that she would witness me starting a new book and then fizzle midway through and give up. It sounds sad and I'm confused because in my life with Ryan, I have 3 books written and am currently writing my 4th. Although they're not New York Times Best Sellers they actually do pretty well and more importantly they make me happy. I love everything about them, especially the book signings and release parties.

I just don't understand why in this life I would give up. It can't have to do with Josh, right? What would a different husband and partner have to do with that? I mean, Ryan is super supportive. Now that I think of it, he was who introduced me to my editor, Isabelle who basically became my agent and booked me my signings and events. So, is that it? Ryan gave me my "in" and Josh doesn't know Isabelle? My brain starts to hurt so I push this thought out of my head for now.

When I arrive "home" Josh isn't there. Shocker. It seems like this dude is never here! Like, how do I even coexist like this? I mean don't get me wrong I love my alone time. In fact, there were times with Ryan I used to actually get annoyed because he would beg me to go to social events with him. I remember one time in particular.

He had been invited to a party with his friends and told me the day of. "Sorry to spring this on you Sweet Pear but honestly I forgot about it. Do you have plans tonight?" I paused and then said, "No, I don't have plans per se..." as I trailed off. "Per se?" He asked with a smile. "Yeah, I mean with other people I don't but I was honestly looking forward to binging Parenthood and eating popcorn and candy. You go though, you don't need me there." "I know I don't need you there," he said as he came up behind me and put his arms around my waist. He nuzzled his face into the space between my neck and shoulder and breathed into my ear, "I want you there. I want to hang out with you." I remember this took me by surprise because it was all I had ever wanted to hear from Josh.

I didn't think it was asking much to hang out with my partner but apparently it was. This moment with my current partner, Ryan showed me how much I had really settled for with Josh.

So, what, I had changed my whole life because of one lousy kiss with Josh? Ok, being completely honest, it wasn't a lousy kiss but it made me feel lousy right after. If I'm also staying on the honesty trail, I'll admit it wasn't the first time I thought of Josh while being with Ryan either. There were times in my marriage, lonely times when I would pluck the good parts of my past relationship and relive them over and over again. I almost perfected the movie reels that played in my mind and made sure to cut to intermission whenever a bad part came through.

I was happy with Ryan but it felt like something had been missing the past year. What was it? Ah yes, passion. He had thrown all of his passion into his career instead of me. Well, didn't I do the same? I threw my passion into my novels with my two lead characters; Justin and Marissa. They were detectives who were fighting their sexual chemistry while trying not to mix business with pleasure. As each book went on, their chemistry rose and I started to realize; I was becoming envious of them. I was jealous of these fictional characters that I had created. They were having these passionate fantasies, while I was married to a man I loved, but our passionate fantasy consisted of sleeping on freshly dried sheets before it reached eleven PM. We had been losing our spark and so I went back to a time I had felt that passion. Cue Josh. All we had had was passion, with a few sprinkles of emotional connection.

When I had that moment with him at the bar it was like I was watching it happen to Marissa, not myself. The alcohol helped yes but it was something I also wanted, as terrible as that sounds. Now that it had, I felt lower about myself than I had ever felt. Spoiler alert- it wasn't worth it and this is not the life I wanted, not by a long shot.

Chapter Eleven

I'm going to get a water out of the fridge when I notice there are flowers on our kitchen counter with a card next to it. What the hell? I think. Maybe Ryan did actually remember me and they're from him? Funny Elle, the thing is, this isn't your novels, this is real life.

I walk over and look at the red roses in the vase and see on the small card it has written, "Ellie." They're from Josh then. "Well, that's a surprise" I say out loud. Guess he learned something and is apologizing for being a huge jerk last night. I open it up and in his boyish handwriting see what he wrote.

> "Ellie, I love you so much. I know I'm not the best husband but I'll keep trying till I get it right, so let's not fight. See, that rhyme there? Anyways, tonight is our night and I'm so lucky to have you in my life.
> Happy Anniversary Ellie.
>
> Love,
> Your Josh"

My stomach drops. Anniversary? Of course, it would be our

anniversary; if there were ever a time for me to pop into this fake life let's make it the wedding anniversary, right? My phone starts ringing and "Babe" is lit up so here we go. "Hello", I say flatly. "Hey Ellie", Josh yells out with cheer. "Are you home? Did you get the flowers and my note?" "I did", I say, trying to perk up my vocal cords. "Thank you." "You're very welcome," he says. "Did you like my little rhyme in there, I should be a poet," he chuckles. Ok, what did I see in this guy? I think to myself. He's not even funny. Play the part, Elle. "Yeah, that was pretty clever," I say. "Listen, I'm sorry but I spaced. I didn't get you a gift this year. Forgive me?"

"Of course, I forgive you Ellie, for a price." Oh, here we go, I think. "Price?" I ask. "Yeah, will you put on that little red dress I love and get ready for me to pick you up at seven?" Red dress? Shoot what red dress? I wonder. I walk into the bedroom and see it draped across the bed. "I laid it on the bed for you", he says. "You've got about 3 hours so go relax and take a bubble bath or pamper yourself however you want and I'll see you at seven."

"Are you already dressed", I ask. "Don't you have to come to our house first, like why would you pick me up?" "Don't you worry your pretty little head," he says. "I've got some things to take care of and I have my clothes with me to change into so see you at seven!"

We hang up and I realize this guy gets me more and more confused by the hour. I call Gwen in a panic and explain the whole phone call. "Gwen, I just don't know what to do. It's our anniversary, I can't sleep with him!"

"Well," she pauses. "Why not? Maybe you can have some fun in this life?" "No!" I scream out. "Just thinking about that makes me feel sick. I've already kissed him while married, I can't continue. My heart isn't with him, it's with Ryan." "I understand," she says with sympathy in her voice. "Here's the thing Elle. I believe you, but I don't know how or when you'll get back to your other life. What if", her voice trails off and I know what she's thinking. "What if I never do," I finish for her. "Yeah," she says quietly. "What if you never do? What if Ryan is seeing someone and he's really happy? What if Josh is your husband for life? I'm not happy about it either but it's what Elle from this life decided. I'm not trying to be harsh with you, I promise. I just don't want you to be looking for the what if, and miss your life here."

"Holy crap Gwen. That's exactly what I was doing with Ryan. I was in this wonderful life with this wonderful husband, happy and successful. Yet, I was always looking to see what if. What if the grass were greener? The grass isn't greener Gwen, it's artificial!" I start crying because I know she's right. This may be my life now. I may have willed away my comfy, loving stable life dreaming and fantasizing about snippets from the past. "It's ok Elle", she says. "Let it out. I'm here and when you're done crying, let me know and we can each pour a glass of wine and pretend we're there to cheers to each other." I take her advice and allow myself to cry more. I sob and let it out, sounding like a high-pitched version of myself and I'm sure for Gwen it's hard to decide if I'm crying or laughing but either way she stays on the line in silence. "Ok", I finally say. "I cried for about five full minutes, that's good enough. I'll get my wine." "Thatta girl" she says. "Ready when you are." "Cheers to us", we say in unison!

Chapter Twelve

I take a look at myself and do a slow spin at my reflection in the mirror and I have to say, I look good! The dress fits me perfectly and I can see why it's Josh's favorite. It hugs in all the right places and just the right amount of cleavage is peeking out. I pair it with dangly gold statement earrings and some nude stilettos I find in my closet. My hair is perfectly curled, makeup is on point and with a spritz of perfume on my wrist and neck, I'm ready to go. I grab my phone to look at the time and it's 7:01. I swear to God, if this guy is late, I'm done. Actually, I'd just go to Gwen's so maybe be late! I look out the window as a black limo is pulling up. No, I think to myself. That is so over the top, that can't be...Josh. He comes out of the limo and is walking up to the front door and actually rings the doorbell!

I open the door and he's standing there with one single rose. He's flashing his signature dimples and I can't help feeling a little bad. He's standing there looking so handsome in his navy blue suit so happy admiring what he thinks is his wife. I mean, to him this is real. He thinks he's in a happy marriage celebrating a milestone and he's trying to impress his wife. This is your mistake, Elle, not his, I tell myself. I have to be a little nicer to him; even if I don't feel it.

"You look unbelievable," he says with his mouth wide open. "I mean, wanna just turn right back around and I'll meet you in the bedroom?" "No", I say with a little laugh. "I want to see what tricks you have up your sleeve. Thank you, you look good too." That part wasn't a lie, he does look good. He's never had that problem; that's been the one constant with Josh. Too good looking for my liking. I always felt I had to be someone else; someone better to get his approval. Not anymore. I decide right there; if I can't leave this marriage and go back to my old life then Josh is going to have to get to know the real Elle. "Are you going to give me that rose or what", I ask. "Uhm... yeah," he says. "Sorry I just can't stop admiring you. Alright you're going to need to walk to that limo in front of me or I won't be able to move from this spot." "Mm hmm" I say back quickly; "or you just want to watch me as I walk away." "Wow," he says. "Well, tonight is going to be some night baby!" He's walking close behind me with his arms out around my waist and I manage to break free and run up the rest of the way. Let me tell you, that is a hard thing to do in stilettos but this version of Elle can do it no problem! He opens the door up for me and "helps" me in by placing his hands on my butt. As he starts to move his hands and massage them, I say, "Ok that's enough. Hands to yourself." I see a moment of shock that's then replaced by curiosity. "Yes mam", he says with obedience. "I'll play along." Oh geez, I think. I have to be careful to be in control of this night completely. No getting drunk because I know what happens to drunk Elle around Josh. I text Gwen too so she keeps me in check. Our code word is "pineapple" if things get out of hand.

We step into the limo and he opens up a bottle of champagne and pours us two glasses. "Cheers to a hot wife and a hot life," he says. "Man, I really should think about becoming a poet!" "Cheers," I say and sip the champagne. I really try to sip it but man, that champagne goes down so smooth. "So, what is it we're doing?" I ask. "Well, Ellie," he says, "we're going to a place my buddy recommended for dinner. They were completely booked; I had to pull a few strings and drop the Anniversary card to get us in! Then later, well that's a surprise", he says as he's about to kiss me. "It's Elle!" I yell out of

SWEET PEAR

nowhere. He pulls back. "What?" "My name is Elle, not Ellie. I know you call me that and honestly, I hate it". "Wha" ... he starts to say and I cut him off. "Yeah, I've never liked it. It's like the only people who call me Ellie are my old teachers, my grandparents when I was little or people that don't respect me. You respect me, right? I mean, I know I never corrected you but I don't like it so please call me Elle from now on." I take a sip from my glass and my heart is racing. I can't believe I just said that. I didn't even realize how it made me feel until it all came out. Man, that felt good!

For a second, I think he's going to yell at me. His face is bright red and he's looking at the driver of the limo like he can hear us. He looks back at me and I brace myself for a rude comment when he says quietly, "Wow, I mean I never knew that. I respect you obviously or I wouldn't be with you but, ok I guess now I know." I almost apologize and then think, no Elle. You spoke your truth; don't apologize to him. Now he knows and that's that. "I just thought it was like our little nickname," he says under his breath. "I'll find something else."

"Yeah, sounds good" I say. I know it came off harsh but it had to be said. "Anyway, what's the surprise later", I ask, trying to change the subject. It takes him a minute to regroup but he refills his glass, chugs it and places it to the side of him. "Oh, that", he says as he gets closer to me. "Well, that, Elle", he says, emphasizing my name in a low tone, "will be a night you'll never forget." He reaches out and gathers my hair over to my other shoulder, exposing my neck as he starts to lightly kiss it. Where's my phone? I think. I need to type Pineapple as fast as I can! P-I-N-E-A, I'm thinking. I glance up as the driver slows down and I've found exactly what gets me out of this aphrodisiac haze. It's a sign. Literally. The sign in front that's looking back at me says, you guessed it, "Sweet Pear". "Oh, we're here", he says happily. "Happy Anniversary Baby!" he exclaims as he lays a big wet kiss on my lips. "Yeah" is all I am able to choke out. Here we go, I think.

Chapter Thirteen

"Hang on, let me snap a quick picture", I say, as I take a picture of the sign and immediately text it to Gwen. I watch as my phone shows the icons for sent, received and then the bubbles showing words typing instantly. "What the actual "?*#***?" she writes back. "Girl, you can't make this up. Forget the safe word. Go rogue, see where this night goes". I read it and don't have time to respond as Josh is ushering me inside.

We walk in and are immediately greeted by the hostess who is searching for our name on the reservation list. I'm too busy scanning the room to see if there's any sign of Ryan that I don't even notice when Josh is saying my name ahead of me. "What?" I ask. "Our table, you coming or what?" he says as he turns back around and keeps walking which leads me to do a little run shuffle to keep up with him. "Are we celebrating something special today?" The hostess asks. "Yes", Josh says proudly. "Our wedding anniversary." "Congratulations" she says with a big smile. "I'll make sure Chef Ryan prepares something special for you." So, he's cooking for us, I think. How odd is this life of mine? My current/not in this life husband is preparing a wedding anniversary meal for my past /ex-boyfriend, current husband and I. Yeah, I'm going to need to order something strong right away.

Our waitress comes over and tells us her name is Lydia and I can't help but notice Josh is looking Lydia up and down. Oh, the old Josh up and down glare. I've forgotten about that one and it seems he has not only continued it into our marriage but on our anniversary dinner of all nights. I used to hate it when we would go places together while we were dating and I would see him not only look at beautiful women up and down, but he would actually sometimes turn around. Hello! Like I can't tell you're checking them out? It caused so many fights and also caused me to have deep insecurities that led to some crazy cleanses to try to lose the most weight in the shortest amount of time. I shudder remembering those times. I hated how he made me feel. I hated how I based my looks and confidence on him. That girl feels like such a lifetime ago.

"Can I interest you in an alcoholic beverage?" Lydia asks with an all too eager smile; not to mention she's only looking at Josh. "You can always interest us"; he says playfully. "What's your strongest cocktail?" I ask. I get a nervous laugh from Lydia and a curious look from Josh. "Wait, Ellie, I was going to order champagne." "It's Elle", I correct him, which makes him blush immediately, "and I'd like to switch from champagne to something else. What if we got a bottle of white? What do you recommend Lydia?" I ask. Lydia nervously turns over her notes in her order book and I can tell that she will no longer be making sole eye contact with Josh. "We have Pinot Grigio, Chardonnay, Sauvignon Blanc and" ... "We'll take your finest Sauvignon Blanc", I announce. "That's ok with you right Josh?"

Josh is looking at me like he's never met me before. To be honest, he really hasn't but I don't care. The rules of the night for me are there are no rules. I'm tired of trying to understand things and just ready to go with whatever it is I'm feeling. "Um, yeah sure Elle, Baby yeah that'll work. We'll take the Sauvignon Blanc, Lydia." I'm about to say I already ordered it but that would be unnecessary. "Sure, I'll go ahead and put that order in right away" Lydia says as she quickly turns away.

"Is Everything ok with you Elle? You came off rude to that poor waitress." Usually, I would have been defensive or even cried at the mere mention that I offended someone or made Josh feel embarrassed by my ungodlike behavior, but not today. "Oh, Josh I'm sorry if you felt that that came off as rude but honestly it's not being rude; it's knowing what you want. I'm not going to dumb down what my tastebuds are craving and if they're craving the finest white then so be it. In fact, that will actually be more beneficial to Lydia as their finest bottle will be much more expensive than a generic champagne, no offense. I mean that in the most respectful way as possible babe. I'll be right back; I'm going to go find the lady's room."

I then get up before I can even see what Josh's face looks like. My plan is to go into the bathroom and laugh hysterically because speaking my mind to him has unleashed this pure giddiness that needs to be set free. I'm looking for the door that says women when I notice the kitchen door is to the left of me. No harm in looking through the window there right? I have to stand on my tippy toes, even in my stilettos and I finally see Ryan.

He's standing in the center of the other chefs holding an enormous pan and flipping the remnants inside like pizza makers do with their dough. I'm watching him laugh with the other employees there and I'm drawn into his energy and the ease he has with making people happy. "Miss, are you looking for the bathroom?" I hear. I look behind me and it's Lydia. She looks nervous still, almost like she's lost all of her confidence. I decide then to do something crazy. "I was actually, thank you Lydia." She points me to the direction and before she walks away, I call out to her. "Hey, I'm sorry if I came off rude to you before. It wasn't you; it was my husband. I mean, this may be TMI but we are out on our wedding anniversary dinner and he was looking you up and down like you're the main course. Honestly, the guy's a jerk and so that's why I ordered the most expensive wine on the menu because I figured if I have to get through another anniversary with him I might as well do it with expensive wine in my glass, right?"

Now, this could go one of two ways. She could think I'm certifiably insane and in turn feel bad for Josh and flirt with him crazily to get to me. Or she could believe what I'm saying and go with girl code. I brace myself as I watch her take everything, I said in. "Oh my gosh girl, I'm so sorry. I was just being nice because he was, I had no idea. For what it's worth, you are absolutely beautiful and deserve better than that." We hug and she promises to take care of me, whatever that means. I thank her, turn into the bathroom, close the door and break out into the laugh that has been building up inside.

Chapter Fourteen

I come out of the bathroom and Josh looks up from his menu. "I was thinking of ordering the oysters for an appetizer; Would your taste buds be ok with that?" He asks playfully. "Yes, that would be fine, thank you" I say. He starts laughing to himself. "What's so funny?" I ask. "I don't know what's up with you today, Elle but you're not holding back, are you? Are you still mad at me for coming back late last night? If you're mad, I get it. I told you I wouldn't do that anymore and I broke that promise so I'm sorry."

This is surprising to me for two reasons. 1.) In all the time we had dated; I never got a genuine apology from Josh. 2.) It looks like in this life there had been a time when he promised he wouldn't come back in the early morning hours like he used to. So, I guess there had been some progression in the relationship? "Well, thank you for the apology," I say. "However, no, I'm not holding back because I'm mad. I've just decided that I'm not going to sugar coat things for you anymore. I'm going to be honest with you about what it is I want and what it is I don't want and if that's something you will have a problem with then we can talk about it." "Ok", he says as he looks back down at his menu. I hear him mutter under his breath; where are these drinks?

It's like Lydia has telepathy as she almost materializes right behind him. "Ok", she sings out. "The finest Sauvignon Blanc for this knockout, and her husband" she says and gives me a little wink. Too much, too soon Lydia I think to her and hope she still has her telepathic skills. "Aw thank you" I say. "She is a knockout, isn't she?" Josh says as he puts his hand on my knee. "I'm a very lucky guy." Neither of us say anything back to him which leaves an awkward silence. She gives me a heavy pour which is almost up to the top and when she pours the glass for Josh it's equivalent to the size of a wine tasting. She then takes the bottle and puts it in the chilled wine bucket and steps back. Josh's eyes are widened as he looks at me like, what is going on? I hold back a laugh and pretend I don't notice.

We order our food and Lydia leaves us back to our own devices. After a few seconds of silence, Josh breaks it. "Ok, so... is it me or is that waitress hating on me?" "What do you mean?" I ask as I bring the glass to my lips hoping I don't spill any because she really filled it up high. "What do YOU mean?" he says. "Look at your glass and look at mine! Mine will be done in half a sip and yours is about 2 glasses worth. Also, she called you a knockout!" "Are you saying I'm not a knockout Josh?" I ask. "Baby, of course you're a knockout", he says; "but it's just weird." "Oh, but it wasn't weird when she was originally paying all of the attention to you huh?" I say. "Then it was me being rude to her; ok I'm understanding." "No, that's not what I meant," he said. "Never mind, you don't understand." No, Josh I think, we don't understand each other.

As the wine keeps flowing, so does the conversation. That was always our scene though. We always were able to laugh and crack silly jokes while getting more and more intoxicated. I decide to be bold and ask a question I'm kind of dreading. "Josh, can I ask you something?" I say. "Course babe," he says. "What's up?" "Why did I give up writing?" I ask. "I mean, you know I write, right?" He laughs a little. "Yeah", he said. "I know you were journaling your stories and stuff but you wouldn't let me read it." "I wouldn't?", I ask with surprise. "I wonder why." "Uh, I don't know Elle", he says as he runs his fingers through his hair. "I mean, you didn't really talk to me about your writing. Oh, except when it's for the bar!" "The bar?"

I ask. "Yeah, the bar I manage, earth to Elle" he says. Ok, so, he manages a bar or owns a bar, I wonder. Well, that's something at least. I'll have to wait to ask which one it is delicately. "So, I know I write for the bar but what's your favorite thing I've written for it?" I ask. This will give me some insight into what I do. "Ummm, he says well I liked *Cupid's soul mate* drink and the *Three's a crowd pleaser* pitcher one was clever too. Oh, what about that other one? I forget the name." As he's searching his brain for the "other one" I realize what I do. I write the drink names for the bar. That's it. In my old life, I have had successful novels and, in this life, I have successfully written names for drinks. Basically, I gave up on my dream because it felt silly to write for me but made more sense to write for my husband's dream.

This has put me in a depressed funk and I can't seem to shake it. If this is my life for good, I need to make some changes, I think. I can be my own creator. I'll do the things I know that will make me happy and writing is definitely one of them. "Well, I'm going to write," I declare to Josh. "Ok", he says. "Then you write baby!", he says as he brings the glass to his mouth. Does he mean to be condescending? I think. Or is that just his overall tone? I don't know Elle, my inner voice tells me, but he isn't your problem. Technically he's your husband but logically and in my heart, not really. His opinion of you means nothing. The only one who is holding you back from success is you! This is helping, I think as I finish my glass and go to pour another.

Lydia brings our meals out and as she places Josh's plate of seabass to him, she announces, "so before I forget; each meal is tailored to each individual person so no sharing is allowed." "What will happen if we share?" Josh asks playfully. "You don't wanna find out," she says back jokingly as she looks my way and flashes a quick, evil smile. "Ok thanks Lydia" I say. "Can we have another bottle of wine by the way?" I ask. "Of course, girl!" she says excitedly as she walks away.

"So, wife", Josh says as he grabs my chair and pulls me close next to him. "I have something very important to ask you", he whispers in my ear. "Yeah? What's that? "I ask, a little nervous to hear his question. "Well," he says so close to my face that I can smell the sauvignon blanc on his breath, "I need to know; what's a guy gotta do to".... As he's speaking, I realize his hand is on my knee under the table and is slowly moving it up under my dress. I should stop him, I think. We're in public and I don't want this to go anywhere further, or do I? I think in a wine infused fog. As his hand goes further and further up to where his finger wraps around the side of my thong he stops and says, "get a piece of your steak." Just like that his hand is off of me and back on the table and I struggle to find my words. "Umm, well that's not gonna happen" I say. "You heard Lydia; the steak is tailored to my needs. Not yours." "Oh baby", he says deviously. "When are you gonna realize, I'm the only one tailored to your needs?" With that he winks at me and pushes back my chair to create space between us.

Chapter Fifteen

This is what he does I realize. He takes my power by being sensual and knowing that I get stuck in his physical spell. It's what he did back when we dated, it's what he did when we kissed at the martini bar and it's what he's doing now. This will never change, I realize. He's able to keep the power in the relationship and do whatever he wants whenever he wants knowing I'll always, always fall for it.

Don't lose you Elle, I tell myself. Remember what Gwen said, he dims your light. You don't want that, your light is the brightest flashlight, I recite in my head. I bite into my steak and it puts the biggest smile on my face. No babe, I think. This steak is tailored to my needs, cooked by my husband. He knows me, truthfully and completely, not you. You know the "perfect" version of me. Ryan knows me and to him it's perfect as is.

At that moment, I hear his voice. At our table. "Sorry to interrupt; but how is everything?" Ryan asks. I look up and see him register my face. "Elle, right? Twice in one day, how crazy." "Ryan" I say, "yes I know, everything is so unbelievably delicious. You are so talented", I say and I mean it so much more than just a single compliment. It's like when we were married, I enjoyed his food but

I also resented it. He was spending so much time at the restaurant he was working at trying to open his own business and if I'm being honest, I wasn't really supportive. Not in the way I should have been. "Well, thank you", he says. "That's really nice to hear Elle".

"Ryan, is it?" Josh jumps in quickly with his hand out to shake Ryan's hand. "Yeah, man this is great. I told my buddies I needed to take my wife to the best restaurant and this place came highly regarded. It's our anniversary today so I needed something special." "Oh, well Happy Anniversary", Ryan says with a quick smile. Does he look disappointed? I think. My heart picks up its pace as I have a glimmer of hope. He redeems himself though and the glimmer of hope is gone. "Well, I don't know if you've thought about dessert yet but, do you like chocolate?" "I love chocolate", I say. "It's my favorite." "I thought so", Ryan said. "Well, if you're open to having a surprise I'll whip up something decadent for the both of you." "I'm definitely open", I say quickly. It comes out sexy and it surprises me. I haven't felt this sexy and confident and wanted someone as much as I want Ryan than I have at this moment. It reminded me of how I felt in the beginning of our relationship. Pretty much our whole relationship minus the past year, I think.

I let myself have a quick moment of indulgence reminiscing about the beginning of my relationship with my husband, my real husband. After meeting him that fateful night when Josh had texted me and I went into full panic mode you would think that's when it all flew into place right?

Not exactly; he was a total gentleman. After I finished my cigarette, he looked me directly in the eyes and asked me an interesting question. "Well, let me ask you something, Elle", he said. My heart started pounding when I heard him say my name. He said it in such a different way. Josh always called me Ellie and he would either say it in a passionate way right before we hooked up or in a way that seemed condescending to me. Little Ellie who doesn't know what to do, little Ellie who would try to be brave but end up shriveling at the thought of Josh leaving her. I felt like he knew I had no power and that turned him on more.

This man, though, said my name in such a different way. He said it in a way that made me feel beautiful. He said it in a way that made me feel confident, like Elle is a big deal. I knew the moment I heard my name spoken that way; I wanted to hear him say it so much more. "What would you like to ask me Ryan", I asked in a breathy tone. "I want to know", he said with a pause, "what you're going to do about this jerk." "Are you going to message him back?" "Ya know", I said with more confidence than I've ever felt in my bones. "I can guarantee to you, I don't need nor do I want to. No, that ship has sailed", I declared as I mimicked a ship sailing far away with my hands.

I saw his body relax ever so slightly. He's into me, I thought. It's not just me imagining this; he feels it too. "Well, I have to say, that makes me feel ..." And that's where he got cut off. For real, I know I couldn't believe it either. Someone from the kitchen called his name and told him he was needed. He shot up and looked at the door and back at me. "I have to go", he said. "I'm really glad I came out here for this break, sweet pear. You made my day." He smiled showing his adorable dimple and went back inside.

"Are you serious?" I said out loud to myself. Now I know what Prince Charming felt when Cinderella cut him off and flew down the stairs without looking back. Who starts a sentence out and says, that makes me feel... oh gotta go, nice to meet ya! He feels what? He feels happy, he feels grossed out, he feels like he has to go to the bathroom, like I get nothing? Needless to say, I walked outside feeling one emotion and walked back feeling a totally different kind of confusion.

So how did it turn into dating you may be wondering? Did we meet again by accident at a bookstore or museum or did I go to see him at the restaurant? Nope, in fact he got my number before I even left the restaurant.

Our server had given us our checks and with it had a little piece of paper folded up. "Ummm" ...Gwen said, as she read out loud. "This is for Sweet Pear", she gushed! "What? Stop", I said, feeling the blood rush into my cheeks. "What does it say?"

"It says", she smiled as she held up the paper close to her face to read and loudly cleared her throat.

"Sweet Pear,

I shouldn't have walked away like that. What I should have done is tell you how breathtakingly beautiful you are and taken a chance by asking you for your number. Since I'm technically in the kitchen preparing meals, which I hope you and your friends enjoyed; I've enlisted Cindy to help me deliver this message. It would be my honor if you would write your number on this paper for me. I'd love to take you out and show you how a real man can treat you the way you should be treated. If I'm not your type, no hard feelings. I just want you to know, I've never had a moment in my life as I did when I first saw you. You really make a guy's heart stop Elle. Go big or go home, right?

-Ryan"

"Ohhhh my God" my girlfriends squealed. "Elle, what happened out there", Lizzie asked. "I told you guys", I said. "I don't know what that is but I know we were meant to meet, that's for sure." "What are you gonna do?" Liv asked. I took the pen, wrote my name and number on the paper and asked for Cindy to come back. "Hey Cindy", I said holding up the paper. "Can you direct me to where the kitchen is?" "Sure honey", she said with a big smile on her face. "What are you doing?" Gwen asked with a devilish grin on her face. "I'll be right back, ladies", I say.

It was like something inside of me was set on fire and I was being led to go with feeling, without thought. She points me in the direction and I go right in. Like I've been in that kitchen many times before. I walk directly up to Ryan. "Uhm, hey dude" the one chef next to him says as he taps him on the shoulder. "What's up?" He asks the guy until he follows his gaze; and then he sees me.

We are looking at each other and it's like no one else is around. It's like when you take a selective focus photo and everything else around you is blurred, clearly allowing you to focus on what you have your sights set on. "Hi" he says in a small, adorable voice and this time it's him who has blood rushing to his cheeks. "Hi yourself",

I say back with that same sexy tone that now seems to be a part of me when I'm around him. "I read your letter; it is the single most romantic thing that has ever happened to me and I want to thank you for that. My number is on there and I wanted to personally deliver it to you." I hand it to him and when I do the tips of our fingers touch and neither of us pull away. I feel the warmth and electricity from him go into my body and it's nothing I've ever felt before. "Well, Elle", he says with a silky voice. "If that's the most romantic thing that has ever happened to you, all I have to say is get ready because I will continue to one up it." "Well, that's a big statement", I say as I pull my hand back. "I look forward to seeing it and you again. Have a nice night Ryan", I smile. I then turn around and walk out, without looking back which is so hard to do by the way.

 I make my way back to the table and feel like the floor is my runway at the powerful woman fashion show. I pick up my glass and finish what's left and say to my girls, "well ladies, that's a wrap!"

Chapter Sixteeen

After we finished eating the decadent dessert that Ryan graciously made for us complementary, we polish off our drinks and proceed to head back in the limo. Josh and I are drunk; like slurring, giggly, the level below the room swirls, kind of drunk. I just about take my seat as he pushes me down and is on top of me trying to kiss me. "What are you doing?" I manage to get out. "C'mon baby", he says. "Let's just do it back here," he says as he's hiking my dress up higher and higher. "I don't even know if you can do it right now" I say, pushing him off of me and smoothing out my dress. "Besides, there's supposed to be a surprise and if that's it, surprise to you, I already know what that's like." "Ouch", he says as he fixes his hair and loosens his tie. "Alright, you get away this time you little tease but when we get back to the room, it's on, like Donkey Kong" he laughs. "Room?" I ask, "What, like a hotel room?" "Oh shoot", he says. "Yeah, hotel. That's the surprise. I booked us a room at the Champagne Chateau", he says with so much pride on his face. It's true, the Champagne Chateau is insanely expensive and drips of romance and well, sex. I have never been to the place but know of people who have. How am I going to turn down being physical with him there? I think. Maybe I continue to get us even more drunk so we go up to the level of spins and then poof, out of commission. Alright, I think two can play at this game. It's on. "Aw, that's so sweet honey", I say. "I'd love another glass of champagne now do we have any more left?" "Patience, baby", he says. "I don't want us to go down the tubes too fast here. There'll be more waiting for us in the room."

Crap, I think. He's onto me. Alright, maybe I can take his mind off of it, I think. "Um...so what's new?" I ask him. "New?" He asks. "Umm ya know nothing. Work is work', he says. "What's new with you?" He asks me back. "Oh" .... I say. "Well, I guess a lot is new really." He cuts me off and looks me in the eyes and says, "you're so beautiful". It takes me back honestly. Is this real emotion coming from Josh? "Oh", I say. "Thank you!" "You really are Ellie", he says and I let it go that he has once again called me a name I asked to not be called. "I'm lucky", he says as he leans over and gives me an honest, sweet kiss. "You are", I say to him and smile. See, this I'm ok with, I think. This is nice and if I'm married to this man for who knows how much longer, taking it slow is exactly what I want. Maybe I can change things this time and make this the relationship I've always wanted with Josh, while I'm still in it, at least. "God you're sexy", he says. "I really can't wait to get back to the hotel". Reel him in, Elle, I think. Reel him in. "Same Josh but can we pause a minute?" "What do you mean?", he asks as he immediately puts himself back into his own space, far away from me. "Well, I mean I just really like this being romanced, wine and dine thing. I don't want to rush into anything too quickly tonight, if that's ok." "Ohhh, I see", he says. "Like a slow build, a super long fourplay? Yeah, I can do that", he says as he takes his fingers and traces them up my leg. "Yes", I say as I cross my legs and grab his hand, "exactly like that. Let's go back to the old days", I say. "The old days, baby we hooked up the first night we met", he says.

He's not wrong. We met at that bar; I had no ride home. The cute bartender offers you a ride home, you take it. It seemed so effortless back then. Girl finds boy attractive; boy finds girl attractive, you get together. There wasn't any wondering if he was interested; he made that very clear right off the bat.

It was nearing time for last call and I had to make a decision on what I was going to do. I saw Josh cashing out all of the other people around me and I still hadn't received my tab. "Excuse me", I called out to him. "Can I have my tab?" "Your tab?", he asked me as he leaned in as close as he could considering there was a bar standing between us. "Gorgeous, you don't have one. I got you covered and now that I will be closing soon, I wanted to see if you wanted to continue this party into a nightcap. What do you say?" He looked me straight in the eyes while a sinister smile started forming at the corners of his mouth, which in turn made me feel instantly warm in all the right places. I didn't even take a moment to think it over, I literally heard the invitation and nodded yes. "Alright then", he said. "Gimme about twenty minutes and I'll meet you outside," he said with a wink as he walked away to finish his shift.

As I got up off the barstool I realized quickly I was very, very buzzed; although I was completely aware of my surroundings and what I was signing up for. I had never had a one-night stand before that didn't turn into a relationship so how would I go about doing this, I thought.

I stepped outside and did some inventory. Legs shaved? Check. Cute underwear on? Check. Lipstick in my purse? Check. I was good to go. Ten or so minutes of sitting on the curb outside of the bar, I started to doubt my decision. What if this guy is dangerous, I wondered. As I'm about to send myself off walking towards my apartment, I feel an arm wrap around my shoulder. "You ready?" Josh asks. I look over at him and see warmth in his eyes. Is this guy a player? I think. Absolutely without a doubt, but he doesn't seem dangerous. He seems like fun, which is exactly what I need at this moment. "Sure", I say, "but look; I don't really know you all that well so I don't feel comfortable going to your house just yet." "Oh", he says. "I get it, you think I'm a serial killer or something? Well, I'm not." "Isn't that what all serial killers say?" I ask. "I mean they're not gonna say, oh man you got me! Yes, I'm indeed a serial killer, so what do you say, wanna come to my house?", I say playfully. "You're a trip", Josh laughs. "Alright, well I do know of this late night/members only bar that stays open later than the two AM call so if you want to get to know me a little better, we can go there.

We are walking down the street to the bar and at first, I'm so nervous I can feel my hands beginning to sweat. Even with my liquid courage I feel very self-conscious in front of this guy. He's just so crazy attractive and I have never been with someone who was literally so perfect looking he could be displayed as a piece of art. We're making small talk and every so often he bumps into me, just ever so slightly but it's enough to pique my interest. He's also the type of person who touches you as he talks. You know those kinds of guys I mean, right? The ones who make it a point to put their hand on your back, or on your knee or shoulder. They find a way to make it seem so effortless on their end but inside your mind is screaming like a schoolgirl in love swooning, "He touched me!"

He slows his pace in front of what I presume is to be the bar, although it doesn't look like it judging from the outside. "Just so you know; I also have friends in here that will vouch for me inside that I'm not a serial killer," he says jokingly with a wild look in his eyes. "Unless you paid them off!" I bantered back. "Hmm, I dunno Ellie", he says, as he runs his fingers through his hair. "That seems like a lot of work and I didn't really have that much time to plan all of that."

He's opens the door and motions for me to walk in when I think to myself, Ellie? I've never really liked how that sounds when it's being said out loud as it makes me feel younger and smaller than I am but I let it go. I'll correct him if he says it again, I think. Now's not the time.

We've been sitting at the bar for maybe a half hour, an hour tops. It's long enough for me to have had two beers and him to have double that amount. I'm becoming aware of how our body language has evolved since we first entered. It started out civil, a little bit of a space between us with me being reserved. It slowly started to change after one beer where Josh told me he couldn't really hear me over the loud music playing so he grabbed my chair and brought me closer to him.

Two beers later and my legs are practically crossed in between his legs as our chairs have both swiveled to be facing each other. I don't even remember when the line was crossed except that I was in the middle of some story when I was cut off. "I'm sorry, I'm trying to listen", Josh said. "I can't concentrate though because all I want to do is kiss you and I can't stop looking at your lips when you talk." It caught me off guard and gave me just enough time to not really think it through and instead I say out loud, "if you want it so bad, go for it!" That really did it. It's like he was a wild animal being held by a leash and his owner whispered in his ear, "go ahead bite that animal, I know you want to."

He put each hand on the side of my barstool legs and pulled it toward him forcefully so that our faces could meet. We were instantly all over each other. Like bad PDA where you don't care nor realize anyone else is in the vicinity. Making out like crazy, hands all over, mine now running through his hair, his running up and down my thighs. It stopped when I heard someone yell from across the bar. "Yo Josh!" There was a man sitting across from us, eating peanuts with a big smirk on his face. "I feel like I should be paying you for this viewing pleasure," he chuckled. Another guy in the group laughs and says "yeah, get a room." Josh and I look at each other, literally panting and catching our breath. My whole body is buzzing, like the feeling when your foot falls asleep and I feel like I'm walking on clouds. I can still feel the indents of where his hands were on my thighs, pulsating. He grabs my hands and says, "should we Ellie, get a room?" "100% yes", I choke out as I grab my purse and he helps me off my barstool.

We proceed to clumsily make out the whole way to his car as he pushes me against wall after wall until we finally find our transportation. While inside the car, we continue fooling around for twenty solid minutes until we get the energy to pull away and head to his house. That night was everything I needed, awakened every desire in me and I was able to be as uninhibited as I wanted knowing this would be a one-night thing. Until it wasn't.

"What are you thinking about baby "Josh asks me as he pulls me back from that flashback. "Nothing" I say. "I guess you're right about us moving so quickly when we first met. I don't want that now though; I miss the courting stage so can we go back to that?" "Yeah, we'll go slow", he says. "Not too slow though, because that just isn't fair, especially on our anniversary" he declares.

Chapter Seventeen

We're putting the hotel keycard in the door and when Josh opens it my jaw drops open. The room looks like it's owned by Christian Grey. It is dripping eroticism, sex and romance. The bed itself is huge and has long white sheer curtains surrounding it and of course there's rose petals spritzed all over. There's a huge heart shaped jacuzzi tub in the corner of the room that's filled with bubbles and petals. On each corner of the tub there are champagne bottles chilling in rose gold ice buckets. There are mirrors everywhere including on the sides of the walls by the bed. I'm walking around to touch the sheets of the bed as they look silkier than anything I've ever felt before and I see a crystal bowl on the end table that's filled with condoms. I walk into the bathroom and see the shower. It's basically the whole room and see-through. There are shower heads on each side with several spots that the water comes out of. Josh is following behind me like a lost dog watching me taking it all in. "Wait until you see the best part Ellie" He squeals. He ushers me back out into the room that leads to the balcony.

I walk out and see that it's not actually a normal balcony but a terrace. This room has its own pool! There's a fireplace out here; I mean this has everything that anyone could ask for. "I didn't bring a bathing suit" is all I manage to say. I look over and see Josh raising his eyebrow and I know what he's thinking. How am I going to get out of this night without any sexual contact, I think.

I can just say no, I hear a voice say inside of me. I know the voice is right. I don't need any reason to say no to my husband if I'm not feeling it. I guess that's the real question, am I feeling it? Would I be feeling it if I weren't married to Ryan? I mean clearly, I was because I kissed him while I was married to Ryan. I need to stop punishing myself for that, I think. That's not the life you're in now. Ryan in this life just sent you off with your new husband. You're not cheating on him. "Well, I'm not skinny dipping so... sorry" I say. "Well, I guess it's a good thing I packed your bathing suit", Josh laughs. "You did?", I ask "where?" "It's in here", he says. "I already checked in earlier today and brought some of your stuff that you'd need." That was sweet, I think. Ok, a little dip in the pool or jacuzzi won't hurt.

I come out of the bathroom in my bikini and see Josh is already in the jacuzzi with two glasses of champagne poured. He whistles as I come out of the bathroom and tells me to join him. I climb in and man does it feel good. The warmth of the water, the silkiness of the bubbles and the scent of the rose petals; it is really nice. He hands me my glass of champagne and leans forward and gives me a sweet kiss. "Happy Anniversary baby," he says. "Happy Anniversary" I repeat back as I take a sip, put my glass down and lean back against the tub to sink into the bubbles.

"How did you get the money to pay for this?" I ask. "What do you mean", he says, "I have money." "I know but this is a lot and with the bar, I don't know I'm just surprised", I say. "Well, let's just say I won a few bets on some games recently so I figured I'd celebrate with my sexy wife." "Oh, cool" I say, as I wonder how much money he really does make at the bar. "Josh, are we ok money wise?" I ask. "I mean, do I need to get a job? Why don't I work?" I ask. "Huh, Ellie, you don't work because I don't want you to, that's my job. I mean, we're going to be making some babies soon." "We are?" I say as I choke on my champagne. "Yeah, I mean, we want to have little guys running around. Or girls, I'm not picky!" "Actually", he says as he comes towards my side of the tub putting his hands on each side of my hips, "we can start now if you want." "No, no" I yell out. "Not yet." "Geez", he says looking hurt. "Ok, it was just an idea. I thought it would be romantic to know we conceived on our anniversary but never mind." "I'm sorry", I say. "I'm just not ready yet to make that decision. I mean, I may want to work."

"Yeah, well let's table that for today", he says as he downs his glass and pours another angrily. I notice he misses the bottle a few times and the champagne goes straight into the tub. I see him take a moment and I legit think he's going to throw up. "Are you okay?" I ask. "Yeah", he says. "I just, I don't know my stomach doesn't feel so good. Um... gimme a minute, I'm going to head to the bathroom", he says as he steps out of the jacuzzi trailing wet footsteps all the way to the bathroom door.

I take this time to enjoy my moment in the tub by myself and continue sipping on the champagne. I realize I've been in here long enough to have my fingers resembling prunes and that Josh is still in fact in the bathroom. I guess I should go check on him and make sure he didn't pass out and die, I think. I knock on the door and just hear a groan greet me back. "Josh, are you alright in there? You didn't pass out did you", I ask. "Nooooo", he says, "I'm just not doing too well in here right now. Something isn't sitting with me well. Can you call and see if the front desk has tums or Pepto or anything baby?" "Sure," I say as I find the phone and call down and order one of each. I put the phone down and think, oh my god... Lydia. Is that why she said not to share and each meal was tailored to our individual needs? Did Lydia poison him? Too far Lydia I think, morbidly too far. Maybe she put laxatives in there? Or maybe it's the mixture of all the alcohol that's been consumed tonight. I honestly don't know how I'm standing and if I should be impressed by my consumption or concerned but this has actually sobered me up. Maybe this is the universe helping me, answering my prayers and taking him out of commission for the night. I start giggling and have to walk out to the terrace so I can laugh out loud in private. "Whatever it was, as bad as this sounds, I am so thankful!" I say out loud as I jump into the heated pool.

Josh comes out a little while later after I have had to open the door and throw in the tums and Pepto. He has a silk robe on and looks like hell honestly. It makes me feel a little bad. "How are you feeling?" I ask as I am now in an identical silk robe in bed drinking champagne and eating a fruit and cheese platter and chocolate covered strawberries, I ordered from room service. "Ugh", he says as he takes a look at my food and turns back around and closes the bathroom door. Shoot, this is bad, I think. "Josh, they have ginger ale in the mini bar, do you want any of that?" "Yeaaaa", he growls out. Open the door, chuck in without looking and close the door in one swift motion is something I have now perfected.

When he comes back out again, he looks a little better. He's less gray and more pale-ish with a hint of color. "Baby I'm sick", he whines as a child would and he literally climbs into bed and puts his head into my lap. I'm stroking his hair and saying, "There, there" as you'd say to a teething, sleep deprived baby. "I'm sorry this is happening," I say. "I know you spent a lot of money for this and it sucks that you're not able to enjoy it." "I'm here with you, so I'm enjoying it," he says in a little kid voice again. "That's sweet" I say, and I mean it. "Wanna watch something on TV?" I ask. "When you're feeling better maybe we can order you some dry toast or something since there's probably not much left in your stomach." "Yeah", he says. "Sea bass wasn't the best thing to come back up." "Ew" I say with disgust. "Ok enough of that talk, drink your ginger ale."

I turn on the TV and we're watching the movie How to Lose a Guy in 10 days; one that I've seen many times but is still a guilty pleasure must have to watch. "This movie is so unrealistic," Josh says while sipping his ginger ale. "How so?" I ask. "I mean, one of them would have said see ya the minute they showed their crazy card. There's no way they'd hold out, even if it were for a bet." "Oh yeah this coming from Mr. Romance himself" I say. "What do you mean?" He asks as he puts down his soda. "No offense man", I say but you don't really lay it on thick with the romance. "Uhm, hello what do you call this?" He says as he motions around the room.

"Ok, good point" I say. "That is true. This night has been romantic, topped off with your countless trips to the bathroom", I laugh. "That's not funny Elle", he says. "I still feel like crap." "I know, I'm sorry" I say. "Really though Josh, I mean this is nice but there are different ways to romance a girl. I mean, name one thing you did in all of our years of knowing each other that you think was romantic." "Besides this?" He asks as he once again over exaggerates his hands to show the size of the room. "Yes, besides this", I say as I prop up the pillows so I can sit up and properly hear what he comes up with. He takes a moment to think and as he does, I decide to open up a new bottle of champagne. I mean it's here; I might as well drink it. 'Ok, I got it", he yells as he snaps his fingers. "Alright, are you ready because this is a good one." "Ready Freddy," I say as I sit back down with my legs crossed facing him.

"I think it was pretty romantic when I texted you after we had broken up and hadn't talked for years. Actually, I called you but you screened it so I had to text." I know exactly what he's talking about, the night I met Ryan. "Ok", I say. "Yeah, I guess taking that leap was romantic but that's the moment you pick?" "Yeah, because I was so nervous that you wouldn't answer me back. I knew I had missed you for a while and I was struggling to message you and finally decided to bite the bullet and go for it. Honestly when you messaged me back; I was so surprised." Huh? I think, message him back? What is he talking about? "What do you mean?" I ask. "What do you mean, what do I mean?" He says. "You don't remember?" He's looking at me like I have three eyes and I realize I have to play this off carefully. "Of course, I remember", I say "but can you tell me how it went down? I want to replay it with your words." Good cover up Elle, I think. "Umm..." he says, "Ok. Well, you wrote back saying what do you want? It was cold and it hurt but I knew I deserved it so I went all out and asked if we could meet up and you obviously said yes because you were out and I met you at your house like an hour later. My palms were sweating and I knew that one wrong move would make you leave for good", he says.

I'm letting him talk and while he is, my mind is racing. So, I messaged him back and I left my girlfriends to meet up with him? I didn't go outside to get some air and I didn't bump into Ryan. I never met Ryan. That's how this life came to be. "You ok, Elle"? He asks with concern. "You're starting to turn gray. I hope you don't have what I have", he says as he passes me his ginger ale. "No, I'm ok" I say. "Go on, I want to hear what you remember from that night."

"Uhm yeah so anyway, you pull up and I get out of my car and we talk out on your front steps, for hours. Your thing was that I would stay out late and not answer your calls and I get that. I get caught up in the moment of being with the boys and one drink turns into another and I don't pay attention to my phone or anything and then before I know it the sun comes up and I know I'm in trouble. I promised you that I would do everything in my power to change. I told you how beautiful you are", he says as he starts to put my hair behind my ears. "I told you I loved you and never stopped loving you", he says as he gently kisses me behind my right ear. "I told you I couldn't imagine my life without you and that I wanted you to be my wife," he says as he then gives me a long kiss on my lips. I feel like I'm in shock as this is all happening and he catches on that I'm not voluntarily acting on this kiss. He pulls away and says with a laugh, "you obviously said no and that was embarrassing but I also told you that I would wait until you were ready. You cried, I comforted you and we made love, a lot", he says as he starts to look at me seductively. "God, I had missed you" he says. "I just remember holding you and touching your soft skin and thinking how lucky I was that you had forgiven me and that you would become my wife, no matter how long that would take. So, yeah baby, I think that's pretty damn romantic if you ask me", he says as he starts to pull on the strap holding my robe together. "I'm starting to feel better too", he purrs out to me as he's pulling my robe down off of my right shoulder.

Chapter Eighteen

I tell him that the room is spinning for me and in all actuality it is. I can't believe this. Not only had I responded to my ex-boyfriend after having no contact for two years but I ditch my group of girlfriends to go meet up with him and have sex with him? What the hell is that? That's so pathetic, I think and I start to feel sick. I can't believe how far I had come and I let it all sink back down because he told me he missed me and wanted to marry me? How did my friends react, I wonder? Gwen must have been livid. I wonder why she didn't tell me this. I can't believe that one move changed the whole course of my life. If I had ignored his messages and didn't jump at Josh's beckon call, I'd be with Ryan.

Josh is actually understanding about me feeling sick so we decide to spend our anniversary night spooning instead. There are some points during the night where he tries to initiate more but I shoot it down by growling out the words, "still sick" or "ew" or my favorite, "I may throw up". That keeps his hands off of me. I just need to buy myself some more time until I know what to do, I tell myself. I can't cloud any feelings for Josh with being physical because it's clear there's been enough clouding going on.

The next morning, I tell him I'm feeling worse and need to get home. He seems annoyed and is only answering my questions with one-word answers but I'm ok with that. I want to get home to make sense of things and to figure out what I'm going to make of this new life of mine.

We get home and I climb into bed pretending to be exhausted and Josh is pacing up and down the hallway clearly wanting out of this house and away from me. "Uhm, Ellie," he says, "I'm gonna head out. The boys are watching the game so if it's cool with you I'm going to go." I've never been happier to be ditched, I think. "No problem Josh", I say. "I'm just going to be in here so stay out as long as you want, really." You would have thought I told the guy he won the lottery. "Alright, thanks baby", he says as he kisses my forehead and just like that he's gone. I stand up to the window and watch his car leave the driveway and call Gwen.

After I spill out to her everything I've learned in the past 24 hours, I take a moment to chug some water and realize I don't hear anything on the other end of the line. "Hello, Gwen," I ask. "Are you there?" "I'm here," she says. 'Sorry, I'm taking it all in. So, this is actually all new to me. You never told me you left our dinner to go with him and you definitely didn't tell me you slept together." "I didn't?" I ask. "Why would I lie to you? I never lie to you." "Oh, I don't know," she says. "Maybe because you knew I would have hit you over the head and told you to run the other way. No, you told us that he kept calling and texting you and you met up with him to tell him to stop but that was weeks later."

"Shoot", I say. "Well, I'm sorry. That's not fair to you guys. I don't know why whenever I'd come in contact with him, it was like I was under a spell and no one else mattered. It's really sad, like who is Elle?" I ask. "You know who Elle is", Gwen said. "I mean, now at least. Elle is a writer, happily married who was having a rough patch. Elle is an amazing friend and Elle is better than Josh Wilson ten times over." "Thank you", I say. "I feel like I've lost her though." "If you feel like you've lost her," she says, "then it's time to find her again."

I get off the phone and keep hearing that sentence in my head. Gwen's right. This is my life now; I don't want to waste years of it thinking about the past. I don't want to waste time trying to decipher why I'm married to Josh. I want to be "selfish" for once and do what makes me happy. What will make me happy is to start writing again, even if I have to rewrite my old books.

    I'm running around the house now looking for any supplies that can work and I make myself a cup of coffee to begin. I start out writing how I used to write all of my books, shorthand. For me that's the best feeling in the world. Filling up my blank pages faster than I can count until I run out of pages. Then I do my second part process where I type out what I've just written. I'm over ten thousand words in when I realize it's gotten dark out and I haven't consumed anything since I started writing. I forgot how in the zone I can be and how the day can literally slip away from me when I'm doing what I'm passionate about. "I'm back!" I say out loud with a grin from ear to ear.

Chapter Nineteen

It hits me one morning that it's almost December and getting closer to Christmas and I haven't gotten a single gift for anyone. I can't really use the "sorry, I thought I was going to jump out of this life back into my old one so no gifts this year" excuse, so I know I need to go out.

I've also successfully managed to keep the physical aspects out of my relationship with Josh. We honestly haven't talked much, probably because I've taken that out of the equation but I couldn't be happier. He doesn't understand nor does he try to understand and that's how I know for sure this isn't the man for me. If you don't care how I'm feeling, then you really don't care for me, in my opinion. It was actually pretty easy. After playing sick for a few days, I told him Aunt Flo was in town and taking her time realizing she was no longer welcome to stay. After that, I plain old told him I was so focused on my writing that I was exhausted. That wasn't a total lie actually. I dreamt, ate and breathed my book. It fueled and ignited me in ways sex with Josh never could and I continue to crave more and more. I'd finish writing past midnight each night and by then I barely had it in me to take my contacts out before bed!

Josh and I were basically roommates at this point. He wasn't home much and I was home all the time and then when I'd go to bed, he'd walk in the front door. We were literally two people next to each other in a revolving door going in the opposite directions. We didn't eat meals together, didn't wake up at the same time and I probably wouldn't even know he was next to me in bed if I didn't wake up to the sounds of him snoring.

I decide to call Gwen to see if she wants to head to the Christmas Market with me so I can get these gifts purchased and put under the tree; that I also have yet to buy. I thought maybe Josh would have brought up the fact that there are zero decorations laid out but there's been nothing.

That part actually shouldn't surprise me. I remember one Christmas when we were first living together. I was so excited to go out and get the decorations, the tree, make ginger bread houses, the whole "Christmas kit". I had this vision dancing in my head (not involving sugar plums) of how our house would look around the Holidays. I couldn't wait for us to make memories that I had dreamt about since I was a little girl. We planned the day we would stock up on our items and decorate the house. I even had it on the calendar as "Josh/Elle Christmas Shenanigans" outlined with a tree. I was giddy with happiness and woke up extra early so that when he woke up, he'd be greeted with a big mug of hot chocolate and topped with marshmallows and whipped cream. We were adults so we were allowed to have whatever we wanted in the morning.

As I was spraying the whipped cream into perfect gloppy swirls on his mug he emerged from the bedroom, fully dressed. "Oh, you're up", I said excitedly. "I wanted to surprise you with a delightful treat. If you play your cards right Wilson, it'll be followed by another equally delectable treat", I said seductively as I shimmied my shoulders and raised my eyebrows. "What are you doing?" he asked with such confusion it completely caught me off guard. He didn't seem interested in my subtle messages and it made me feel embarrassed and silly. I saw then that he was grabbing his car keys and the realization hit me.

"What do you mean", I shrugged while I tried to gain my composure back. "It's our Christmas Day remember? We have it on the calendar." I pointed over to the calendar with one hand while my other gripped the mug meant for him so tightly. It was burning hot beneath my fingers but I didn't even feel it anymore. I felt numb. "You didn't forget right?" "Oh ...", he paused. "Ellie, I thought that was a joke. I mean, do you really need me to help you decorate the house? I thought that you'd want to take care of that; I don't have that artistic eye that you do." As he said this he came over and gave me a kiss on my forehead. "Is this for me?" he asked as he grabbed the mug from my hand. "Thanks babe, that's so cute!" He took a sip from the mug, winced at how hot it was and then placed it next to the sink. He was done with it.

My heart sank. It really felt like it left my body. I immediately felt like a child. Like we were never on the same page, even though I thought we were. Did I imagine this? No, I remember we even talked about what colors we would pick as our scheme.

"Well, I ...." I started to say but my voice left me for a moment. "I can't get a tree by myself. I would need help." "Oh yeah, well of course Ellie," he said warmly. "I can do that for you. How about this? I have to run over to Jacob's for a little bit but when I come back, we can go and do that? I'm not like leaving you high and dry, I just don't really think I need to be here for the shopping and decorating part. You understand right?" I started to say sure even though I don't even know how that word was formulating in my mind. I didn't feel sure. Instead, I just kind of froze. "Are you mad at me? Oh, geez Elle, now you're going to make me feel bad. I don't need this right now. I have so much stress at work and other things to deal with. I'll see you later, I'm outta here." He said this all with such frustration and anger and I had no idea where it came from. It scared me because it made me feel like maybe I was being too much. Wanting too much. I was pushing him away.

"No, no, wait Josh!" I said finding my voice again. "I'm not mad at you. Don't leave like this." I grabbed him by the arm and pulled him back to me. His eyes looked at me with anger and I watched as they slowly started to return back to neutral. "It's fine Ellie, I'm not mad at you either. I love you. I'll see you later and we'll do the tree thing. If the offers still on the table, maybe we can partake in the "delectable treat" you were talking about earlier?" As he said this he leaned in and kissed my neck, tenderly and then with more force. As my body started to respond before my mind could catch up, he pulled back and lightly kissed my mouth. "Bye babe", he said quickly and before I could even react the front door closed.

I remember I stood there for a long time. Not moving, not reacting, nothing. Then the questions filled my brain. They swirled by so fast it felt like pressing fast forward on a movie and when you went to play it again, you lost your place. Once the questions stopped the emotions started. I heard the sound of my sob erupt from my throat before the tears came. I cried hard and for a long time. I ended up sitting in a fetal position against the wall until the moment of silence came. That was my cue to get up, wipe my tears away and grab a tissue. After I erased the evidence of emotions from my body, I picked up the mug of hot chocolate and it was no longer warm. I took the biggest gulp and grabbed my purse to get my own decorations. That Christmas we had no tree, but we had the best god damn decorations.

That memory hurts me all over again but in a different way. Now, I look at that girl and I feel so sorry for her. How dare that boy make her feel less than about herself. He made her feel like an idiot and silly when he was the one afraid to experience real joy. He was afraid of closeness and making memories. He gaslit me before that term was easily accessible to find out about online.

I realize I'm still angry. I let myself process those emotions all over again and instead of drowning in them, I let them fuel me. I'm not that girl anymore Josh. I don't "need" you to help me get a tree. I don't "need" your input for decorations or gifts. I don't "need" you or anyone to deplete me.

No offense to Gwen but I decide against calling her. This memory I've revisited puts a palpable shift inside of me. Time to take on the Christmas expedition on my own; I think to myself.

I get into my car and put on the radio and of course a holiday song greets me on every station. Christmas was always my favorite holiday before and I actually have beautiful, movie moment memories with Ryan. It was the exact opposite as my time with

Josh. Now though, I feel nothing for the holiday. It's more about just going through the motions. It's really sad that I feel zero connection to it. I've got to make an effort, I think. Yes, your life right now is in disarray but maybe it's time to take the men out of the equation. Christmas makes YOU happy so embrace it! I start singing along to the songs as they come on and it does help. Singing these old-time songs reminds me of being a kid again when the magic of Christmas was something special I felt within. The drive feels like it was merely minutes and suddenly I've arrived.

As I get out of my car, I notice the Christmas Market is huge! I've come here for many years but it's gotten so much bigger as time goes on. It's filled with local, small business vendors that are displayed around the town. They literally close off the streets so that you can just walk around on the sidewalks taking in the sights and beauty of Christmas. The smell of pine and roasted nuts fills the air and I can't help but take a huge whiff. There are tea lights strewn across the tops of one building going all the way across the street to the other and it makes it look so magical and whimsical. I take a moment in and let myself look around and bask in the magic of this time of the year. There are so many different businesses here and a ton of people are crowded around. It can feel a little overwhelming trying to navigate where to go first; so, I decide to start at the stand that has the extra-large thermoses of hot chocolate. At the last minute, I also decide to splurge on a chocolate-chip peppermint cookie. Tis' the season, right?

Hours later and many loops around the streets, I have huge shopping bags filled and stacked on each arm. I've purchased gifts for everyone, including Josh. I managed to find his favorite cologne and that's a win in my book. It would look rather rude if come Christmas I had no gifts for my "husband". I'm looking at beautiful hand carved Christmas Angels while trying to juggle my bags and one of the bags slides off my arm and hits the ground. "Crap!" I say out loud as I pray it wasn't the bag with the snow globes. As I'm crouching down to assess the damage, I hear someone next to me ask, "Need a hand?" I know who it is before I even look up and with a huge smile, I can't seem to hide, I say, "Ryan, hi, what are you doing here?"

"Hmm" he says playfully. "Well let's see, it's almost Christmas and I'm at a Christmas market so I guess it's fair to say I'm being a last-minute Christmas shopper. Nice to know though I'm not alone", he says as he motions to my bags while bending down and handing me the one that fell. "Hey now", I say. "Nothing wrong with being a delayed shopper. It just means you like the pressure." "Oh, is that it", he says with a laugh. "Well, you're not wrong there. I do my best work when I'm under some pressure." There's a moment where we just gaze at each other as we both realize how that sentence takes on a different meaning and it's not the cold that's given us rosy cheeks.

"Anyways", he says, as he clears his throat, "I do actually have a problem that maybe you can help me with." "Oh, what's that?" I ask, with genuine curiosity. "My mom", he says. "I have no idea what to get her at all for Christmas. Maybe you can help?" "You're not doing the ornaments?" I say before I can stop myself. I shouldn't know any of this information as I technically haven't spent many years with his family on Christmas morning, knowing we always get his mom the newest Christmas ornament. "Huh?" He asks, looking puzzled. "Oh, nothing" I say. "I know moms tend to love ornaments but, do you not get her that usually?" "No", he says. "Usually, my brothers and I go all in on a gift but they're married now so I can't really fifth wheel it with them." "Oh, you're not married?" I ask while bracing myself. My heart skips a beat as I realize that maybe there's a chance. "Nope, no ring", he says as he shows me his bare hand. "I was in a pretty serious relationship though that looked to be going that way but that didn't work out", he says as I notice he looks to be deep in thought. "Oh, I'm sorry to hear that", I say. "Her loss, really though, unless you broke up with her. I'm sorry I shouldn't have assumed", I say as I struggle to place my bags up higher around my arms. They're getting heavier by the minute and starting to cut off my arm circulation. "Here, let me", he says as he grabs the bags from me and holds them as if they're filled with feathers, instead of rocks. "Thank you", I smile. It's clear to me he doesn't want to talk about this past relationship and instead of bringing the mood down, I change the topic. "Ok, so tell me a little bit about your mom; what does she like?"

It's a difficult thing to listen to someone talk about their family members that you know like the back of your hand. Sherri is really like my second mother. She's always been so warm and inviting and it was like that from the first moment I met her. That's another thing that's made it so hard being separated from Ryan. I'm also separated from his mom, dad and two brothers. You'd think it would be hard to fit into a family with three boys but I became the little sister instantly. They liked picking on me and I loved dishing it back. I'm an only child so I never had that sibling rivalry. Ryan loved it because instead of him being the baby of the family getting ganged up on; he now had something to bond with by joking along with them. I love hearing about Ryan's family though from his mouth. He mimics them perfectly and it takes everything in me to not tell him so. I also get to hear about the other pieces that I never got to experience; like his brothers getting married. When I was married to Ryan, his brothers Zack and Garrett were still living the bachelor life. It's odd how taking me out of the equation has changed it so they not only got out of that phase but also found their other halves and are happily married.

Ryan's telling me all of the things his mother loves: gardening, cooking, decorating for the holidays, the typical mom things. "I don't know", he says. "Maybe I'll just get her a new phone; she's been due for an upgrade for years but hasn't gotten around to it." "That would be nice", I say "but what if this year you did something more meaningful? What if you made something", I say as the idea suddenly comes to me. "Made something?" He says, "like what, dinner? I actually cook for them all the time so that's not really different." "Not what I have in mind" I say with a smile as I gaze over at the Wreath stand sign that says, "Make your own homemade wreaths". I see Ryan follow my eyes, squint to read the sign and say, "oh hell. Well, Christmas is only once a year, right? Let's do it."

We are sitting at the benches next to the Wreath stand and ours is just about complete. "It looks really beautiful Ryan", I say as we both hold it back to admire it. "This is something I would have never thought of or done", he says with a chuckle. "She's definitely going to be surprised. I didn't realize you were so creative. What is it that you do? I don't even think I asked before." "Well," I say, "I used to be a writer. I took a little break after getting married but now I'm getting back into it." "Really?" He asked. "What do you write?" "Fiction mystery," I excitedly said, realizing how just saying that lights me up. I told Ryan about my characters and how ironic it is that their biggest mystery is within themselves.

"I love it", he says when I finish telling him the premise of my first book. "Really?" I ask. "Thank you. It feels so good to be writing again. I don't know if anything will come of it but it's just so much fun to tell the stories of my characters." "I can tell", he said. "Your whole demeanor changed when talking about it; like how I get with food. It's your passion Elle, don't ever give up on that." "I won't", I say out loud. I won't ever give up on myself again, I think to myself with a smile.

"I actually have these regular customers of mine that are book publishers. I could put a good word in for you if you'd like?"

"I'd love that! "I say excitedly. "You don't have to do that though; I don't want to put you through any trouble. Plus, what if you think my writing actually stinks and put your name on the line to recommend a crappy author?"

"Well, I find that hard to believe", he says sweetly. "I don't get the vibe from you that anything you do would be crappy and it's not a trouble at all to me. I love networking talented people in my life. Actually, I think they may be in the reservation book coming up soon. Maybe, I should get your number in case they're interested and I could give them your info?"

I feel my heart flutter. He believes in me, without even knowing me. God, he's such a good guy. Not to mention, he's asking me for my phone number! Not in the way I may have hoped, but hey, it's still a step.

"Sure", I say as I motion to grab his phone. I'll type it in for you and then you can text me so I have yours. So, then I know who it is that will be getting in touch with me, I mean", I say quickly. I don't want him to think I'm trying to get his number. "I knew what you meant," he says quietly and smoothly.

I watch his eyes sparkle and his mouth breaks out into a side smile as he gives a quick laugh and hands me his phone. I add my name in as only "Elle" and type my number in. "Sorry, I should have written my last name. You may have other Elle's in your phone for all I know."

"Nope, no other Elle's in my life", he says as he's typing. His voice and words make me melt. He has no idea what kind of effect he has on me. I hear my phone beep and I pick it up as if I've forgotten I told him to message me. His number pops up and the message from him says, "Ryan. Don't know if I should have put a last name or not?" It's followed by an emoji of a happy face with the tongue sticking out.

"Nope", I repeat back to him. "You are the only Ryan in my phone and life as well." "Well, look at that", he says as he nudges me with his arm. "Each other's firsts." We both then nervously laugh and it turns into us both giggling as I adjust the bow on his wreath.

"Alright, he finally says after we've collected ourselves. Do you have time to help me pick out gifts for the rest of my family?" "There's nothing more I'd rather do", I say. He laughs as he thinks I'm being sarcastic but inside I've never been more honest.

Chapter Twenty

After we've walked around to basically every vendor; I've refilled my thermos with hot chocolate and both of our arms are now filled with gifts, I realize it's time to get home. I really don't want to; it feels so effortless to be with Ryan. As much as I'm enjoying his company though; I'm also enjoying the idea of getting into my comfy clothes, pouring a glass of wine and continuing my book. Ryan insists on walking me to my car even though I've told him I can handle carrying the bags myself.

"I'm really glad I ran into you today Ryan", I say. "I am too, Elle", he replies as he's finished putting my bags into the trunk of my car. "Don't worry, I won't take all the credit for my mom's gift; I'll be sure to tell her that a very nice lady helped me." "A very nice lady?" I say. "Ouch, that makes me feel old." 'Well, I don't think it would be appropriate to tell her a very nice, very beautiful but also married lady helped me", he says and I can tell instantly that he didn't mean to say that but it just came out. "I'm sorry; that was pretty inappropriate to say" he spouts out quickly. "It's ok, it's nice to hear a genuine compliment," I say. "Not inappropriate at all." "Ok, good", Ryan says. "Sometimes I forget to have a filter and this was definitely one of those times. Anyways, have a wonderful night Elle and if I don't run into you again soon, have a Merry Christmas." "You too Ryan", I say. "Merry Christmas."

    I turn around to get into my car. As I close the door, I'm able to let out an audible sigh. "Holy crap", I say quietly to myself. I start my car and it makes a little ticking noise but doesn't start. I try again with my key. Same thing, radio comes on playing that Christmas music but the ignition doesn't catch and keeps making that ticking sound. "No, no, don't do this to me," I say out loud. I hit the steering wheel in frustration. I see Ryan turn around and look in the car at me. I can tell he's probably thinking the same thing as we definitely had an awkward goodbye exchange. I try one more time, tick tick, nothing. I look over at Ryan and put my hands up and shake my head no. I open the door and Ryan looks concerned. "Car not wanting to leave?" He says. Not just the car, I think. "Doesn't seem like it wants to", I say. "I do have tow insurance but I have so much to do and I don't feel like waiting around for them to get here. It's getting dark too." "Give me a minute", Ryan says quickly as I see him sprint back into the market. Was there an Auto store at the market I missed? I think. He comes back a few minutes later and motions for me to come out of my car. "Ok, here's the deal", Ryan says. "I just talked to Betty at the ticket station and she said it's perfectly fine to leave your car here overnight if you need to. I can give you a ride home or to your husband if you want and then tomorrow you can call the towing company when you're ready for them to meet you here. I know it's getting close to dinnertime and I can spot a hangry female a mile away", he says with a little laugh.

    "Are you sure?" I ask. "You don't have to do all of that; I mean I really appreciate that but that's asking a lot of you." "Not really", he says. "The perks of owning your own restaurants are you can adjust your hours if need be. I checked in with my sous chef earlier today anyways and he's got it covered. So, Elle, if you need my help I'm here." "Alright", I agree. "Let me call Josh first and see what he wants me to do." "Sure", he says. "That's probably the best thing to do. I'll wait around just in case."

    I call Josh and it rings four times before going to voicemail. I send him a quick text that says, "Hey I'm at the Christmas Market.

My car won't start. Should I come to you or go home?". I wait a few minutes while making small talk with Ryan. "If you want, we can just swing by where your husband works", Ryan says. "If he wants you to go home, I don't mind taking you there and if he wants to take you then problem solved, either way."

"Alright, that sounds like a good plan", I say. I get in Ryan's car and I'm not surprised with how clean it is. He was always a little neat freak with things like that. "Did you just buy this car?" I ask. "No, I've had Lena for about two years now" he says while he taps the steering wheel lovingly. "Why do you ask?"

"Well," ...I say, "First of all; I won't even get into the fact that your car's name is Lena but it also smells brand new. How is that even possible?" "Well, I take good care of the things I love", he says. I watch him smile and see the crinkles that form on the sides of his eyes and it takes everything in me not to lean over and kiss him. I have no clue how our physical intimacy seemed to fizzle before. I look at him now and I can't stop thinking of all the ways I want to show him my love. His smile, his beautiful crystal blue eyes, his scent, I love everything about him. I took this man for granted, I realize. Even now, I'm a complete stranger to him and he's dedicating his time to help me. We pull up at the bar Josh works at and Ryan and I get out to see if he's there and able to talk to me.

We walk in and there's a few customers at the bar but one in particular catches my eye. I see a younger woman wearing a cutoff denim skirt and a very low-cut pink tank top giggling while Josh is practically leaning over the bar to whisper something into her ear. She has her hand on the inside of his arm almost pulling him in closer. It looks bad, really bad and I can hear Ryan exhale out a deep breath. I look over at him and try to hold it together. "That's your guy, right?" He asks with concern and a hint of anger. "It is", I say, holding back tears.

It feels like an eternity we are standing there and it's hard to believe that Josh can't even sense that two people are staring at him so intently. I just watch them for a moment as she has her hands all over him and his body language is telling me that he enjoys it. It reminds me of the time that we first met and makes my mind start to spiral.

I feel my face getting hot, but not because of jealousy. I'm more so embarrassed that this is happening while I'm here with Ryan. I mean, if this isn't the definition of irony, I don't know what is. Ryan then clears his throat, breaking me out from my frozen haze. "Uhhh, what do you want to do?" He asks me, trying to sense my emotions. "I want to leave", I say. "Can we do that? Can we leave?" "Of course, we can", he says as I hear the girl say, loudly and slurring might I add, "you're so bad Josh"! As I turn around and walk ahead of Ryan, I hear Josh loudly question, "Ellie?" "Hey Ellie, wait!" Ryan stands close behind me so Josh can't see me anymore and he turns back around to look him in the eye as he places his hand on the small of my back and leads me outside.

Chapter Twenty-One

I'm running back to the car as I hear Ryan now yelling out my name. "Elle wait! You're gonna get hit!" I somehow manage to dart through the traffic and make it to the passenger's side door before I put my hand on the side of the car and start crying. I let out all the emotions I've been feeling since I entered this backwards world. Of course, Josh would cheat on me. I mean, I suspected it for years when we were dating, why would I think being married to him would make it any different? This is my ultimate karma. I cheat on my loyal, amazing husband with this jerk and end up married to him, to have him then cheat on me! It's what I deserve honestly.

"Elle, are you ok?" Ryan asks as he catches his breath looking down at me with such concern in his eyes. "What can I do? I'll go back in there if you want and give that idiot a piece of my mind!" "No, no", I say while wiping my tears away with my sleeve. "He's not worth it, trust me!" "Elle, anyone that would ever cheat on their partner is no good. Especially someone that would cheat on you, I really mean that", he says while he pulls me in for a hug. His attempt to console me makes it worse as I realize he's talking about me without even knowing it. I continue ugly crying and wiping snot off of his sleeve and he lets out a little laugh and says, "don't worry about it, it's laundry day today anyways."

This makes me laugh and I'm able to take a minute to pull myself together a little more. "I'm sorry Ryan" I choke out. "Sorry? for what?", he questions. "For anything that ever happened to you that hurt you. You're an amazing man and if someone didn't appreciate that or see that, they're blind." I watch his face get a little red and I can tell I tugged on a heartstring. "Elle, thank you" he smiles. "You should know though, what you just said to me, is exactly what I think of you too. I don't know the details of your relationship but I do know what we just saw in there isn't ok. You're allowed to be upset."

I put my head back on his chest and we embrace once more. This time we hold onto the hug a little longer, appreciating each other's hearts and company. After a moment of neither of us talking, he speaks right next to my ear and says, "You, ok?" I feel the hair on my neck and arm stand up. He's got my body's full attention. "No, but I will be," I say as I wipe the tears from my eyes. "Do you want to get back in the car or stay here? I'm game for whatever you want to do." "Let's get in the car and leave," I decide. He opens my door and lets me in and I close it looking out the window at the bar and thinking to myself, yeah, this chapter is done.

Chapter Twenty-Two

"Alright, so ... what would you like me to do?" Ryan asks as he taps on the steering wheel. "I can take you home if you want to be alone or I can take you out to dinner, not in a romantic way", he laughs, "but to fill your belly. Whatever your wish is, I'll make it happen." "What about work? Don't you have to go in?", I ask. "Hang on", he says as he presses a button on his steering wheel and I hear ringing through his speakers. "What's up boss?" I hear a male voice answer. "Hey Trev, are you ok to be head chef tonight? I'm not going to be able to make it in." "Uhm sure boss, is everything ok?" He asks with concern. "Yeah man everything's fine. I have a friend that needs me, so this takes priority." My heart burns as I hear him talk to his employee. He thinks of me as a friend! His employees seem to genuinely care about him and they don't question his loyalty.

After he hangs up, he looks over at me and says "ok Elle...what's your last name again? I actually forgot." "Ya know, let's go with my maiden name. It's Green, Elle Green." "Whoa ok", he laughs. "Elle Green, where would you like to go tonight?" "This might sound strange", I say "but...what would you say about going to the movies? I noticed before the theatre down the street is playing Home

Alone and it's one of my favorite movies." He flashes that dimple that makes me weak in the knees and says, "Miss Green, we have something in common. It's my favorite Christmas movie too. Your wish is granted!"

    Truth be told, I know it's his favorite movie. We watch it every December together. Sometimes three times in a row, seriously. Honestly, we even put it on when I'm feeling a Christmas in July nostalgia too. We can recite every quote in that movie from "I made my family disappear " to "Keep the change you filthy animal". It's our movie! I am so excited, practically skipping while we are in line for our tickets. He's looking over at me laughing and it almost feels like we are together again. I stop him once we have the tickets in our hand. "Ok, so, here's the thing, Ryan. When I go to the movies, I like to get popcorn, candy and a soda. Is that cool with you? If it's not, this movie moment isn't going to work out for me." "Ooh", he says as he pretends to be contemplating. "It's cool with me as long as you get butter on that popcorn" he says with a smile. "Also, I need pretzel nuggets with cheese so let's go crazy!"

    He pays for everything, despite me offering. "Look when you're being consoled, you get free stuff ok? Deal with it", he says. I love this dominant personality he's showing me. I forgot how hot he can be when he's confident. I let myself wonder what would happen if I just grabbed his hand right now and held it. Would he pull away or would he let it linger there as we both felt the electricity course through our fingers, then through our veins as we can't stop from becoming magnetic, letting our bodies press up against each other. "Did you hear me?" He asks. "Huh, sorry my mind was somewhere else", I admit. "I can tell, your cheeks are flushed," he says as he points to my cheek with his hand. "I asked if you wanted coke or Sprite". "Sprite" I choke out. Shoot, he knows, I think. He has the cutest smile forming on the sides of his mouth. He must have been able to see I was fantasizing. Is he flattered? He hands me the soda and popcorn while he balances his drink and pretzels in one hand and with the other ruffles my hair and says, "it's theatre #3 blusher." "I'm not blushing!" I yell, as I take a few steps ahead of him and run to the theatre. I can hear him laughing behind me and it's become my favorite sound.

We find our seats in the back and I notice that there's only one couple that's in this theatre. "Sweet", I say as I nudge Ryan. "We basically have the whole place to ourselves." "You better behave yourself!", he teases. "I want to watch this movie so if you do something to get kicked out, I'll see you outside when it's over." "I promise I'll be good", I joke back with him as I can't erase the smile that's formed on my face.

As I grab my cell phone out of my purse to turn it off; I see I have four missed calls and a slew of texts that are all of course from Josh. "Ugh", I say out loud. "What is it?" Ryan whispers. I show him my phone and take a sip of my soda. "Do you want to call him back?' He asks. "No, I don't. I honestly don't know when I will want to speak to him. He can wonder where I am for once" I declare, as I turn off my phone and put it away. "Well, I know you're not asking for my opinion here but you know what they say, two wrongs don't make a right. He obviously wants to talk to you so maybe hear him out? See what he has to say? It could have been a big misunderstanding for all you know?" "You're right Ryan", I whisper back. "I didn't ask for your opinion." I throw some of my popcorn at his face. "Oh, you want to start a war huh?" He says loudly as he grabs a pretzel nugget to throw at me. "Shhhhh", I whisper. "The movie's about to start." I see him open his mouth to reply back but then decides to throw the pretzel nugget in instead.

We're about a third of the way into the film when Ryan nudges me. I look over confused and see him looking at me with a devilish grin. "What?" I mouth to him with my brows furrowed. He signals with his head for me to look in front of us to the right. I follow his gaze and see it. There is the only other couple that's in the theatre with us, making out. They look to be pretty young; I'd guess in high school or early college days. They're really going at it too, like they don't even realize they're out in public. "Oh my God!" I whisper to him as I place a piece of buttery popcorn into my mouth. He raises his eyebrows and starts laughing and I am covering my face as I suddenly feel shy. He grabs my hands trying to pry them away from my face. We're both laughing hard and I think he's pleased with himself that he's taken my mind off of everything for the time being. I feel hot all over; thank God the lights are low because I'm sure that my face is as red as a tomato.

It's then that we watch the girl roll over from her seat and literally straddle the guy. "This is a great movie! Should be rated a little higher than PG-13 though." Ryan says unable to control his laughter and we both reach into the popcorn tub at the same time. Our hands touch and we look up at each other. There's a brief moment I see something in his eyes glimmer. Is it intrigue? It's definitely a look I've seen before from him and my body instantly responds remembering what that look usually led to.

I imagine running my fingers slowly up his hand and arm, taking my time tracing my way up to his bicep. I can almost hear the moan come from his mouth as I guide my hand up around the side of his neck and let my fingers dig into his hair. I sit in this moment for a minute, massaging the back of his head as I watch his legs tremble. I can feel the warmth of his body pulsing as I lean in and kiss his neck, and sense him twitch as I lightly breathe into his ear. I watch him turn then and look at me with his mouth slightly open, his lips slightly swollen and his eyes glazed with lust as he grabs my face with his right hand and kisses me with such passion; I feel like I'm going to pass out.

Now it's me who twitches and I realize, crap, I was indulging in a fantasy again and now I've snapped back to the present moment. Why do I keep letting this happen? He's going to think I'm a lunatic, like how much time has even passed? He's looking at me inquisitively and I feel really awkward like he was maybe able to see into my thoughts. I don't know what to do so I decide to lighten the mood by smacking his hand out. "Alright, alright it's all yours." he laughs. I wish I was all yours, I think. I rearrange how I was sitting and use my napkin to fan myself quickly as my face feels like it's on fire.

My eyes can't stop darting back to the couple and as I'm watching them be carefree and completely uninhibited, I feel myself going through all types of emotions.

Number one: I feel embarrassed. There's a feeling of an elephant being in the room (or theatre) knowing that on my end at least, I have sexual tension with Ryan. Have you ever felt your fingertips and body buzz without the person next to you even touching you? I have and it's happening right now. I can't say why but I literally feel like if I were to look to my right at him, he would be turning to the left at the same time. I can feel our charged energy and the situation in front of us, which seems like it's heading to second base, isn't helping. I won't let myself look over at him, even though I feel his presence heavy next to me. I try to focus on the movie but I find myself continuously glancing over at them.

Number two: I feel jealousy. I'm jealous that they're able to display their feelings of wants and desires so publicly and passionately. They're so young and they have their whole lives ahead of them. Passion is literally pinned to them, like a nametag. Their hormones are all over the place and they seriously can't help themselves. Every place they go to has a scent of pheromones wafting; everything their partner does is an aphrodisiac. The way their partner's mouth moves when they talk. The feelings they get when a piece of their clothing brushes against the other person's body; hell, even the way their breath smells to each other is instant foreplay. I'm jealous that that's gone for me, or at least I thought it was. I didn't think I could have that again with Ryan so I sabotaged it and ruined it. I ruined us. I let it all just slip away thinking it was hopeless and instead redirected my passion onto someone else, someone way less deserving.

Number three: Sadness. This one is the hardest. I'm brought back to moments of nostalgia from our relationship. I miss us. What we had was so damn special. Even this very movie is so special, well, was so special to us.

I'm brought back to the times we would start the fireplace and snuggle up in our oversized plaid Sherpa blanket while fighting over who ate more popcorn that was supposed to be divided equally. I would get hit with a pillow if I said the lines before the character got to them and he would get pinched if he reenacted the moment when Macauley Culkin throws his hands up to his face and screams. I miss the comfort of it all. I really did blow all of this; he's too good for me. It's not lost on me that we're here together, watching this movie, and I can't even touch him. I wanted to badly to see him once I woke up next to Josh and now that I'm here I feel miles away. A tear runs down my cheek as I come to a realization. I know now what I need to do.

Chapter Twenty-Three

We're exiting the theatre and I can tell he can sense that my mood has shifted. We've been driving for a few minutes in silence when I hear him clear his throat. "So should I ask you if you're ok or do you want to internalize?" he asks as he adjusts the radio station. "A little of both", I say with honesty. "I'm not surprised by Josh and this isn't the first time I've suspected him acting shady. I've questioned his faithfulness for a while so this is the push that I think I needed. I'm not happy in this relationship and I haven't been for quite some time. I know it's not worth saving because it doesn't fulfill me. I know that may sound a little harsh, but it's the truth and I need to do what's best for me solely." There's a little bit of silence so I decide to go for the jugular.

"Also, if I'm being brutally honest Ryan, I know it's not worth saving because I know now what is worth it. This will sound crazy so brace yourself. I know we just met and don't know a whole lot about each other but I like you. I know I shouldn't say that and I know I shouldn't feel that but I do. Your presence and company feels right and comfortable and safe, which is how it should be. I know though that nothing good comes from acting on those feelings, especially being in a marriage. So, even though it's the furthest thing I want to do; I have to distance myself from you as well, at least for now. You're a little bit of a distraction and I have to make things right within myself before anything can come to fruition." I sit uncomfortably in silence for a few seconds which feels like an eternity and I make myself look over at him. He's gripping the steering wheel so I know that means he's nervous. It's hard to tell if he's blushing in the car so I don't know what emotion he's feeling. "Any thoughts?" I ask.

"Any thoughts", he repeats back to me. "Well, I respect the hell outta you," he says quietly. "You're right; acting on those feelings isn't the right route to take. People get hurt. I know because it happened to me. Not to get all into the past but my last relationship ended with her being unfaithful and it was hard to navigate through that, really hard. You knowing that, even after witnessing your husband crossing that line himself, shows your character. Then hearing you say what you feel about me, well that's the nicest thing anyone has ever said to me. I would be lying if I said it wasn't reciprocated and that scares me more than you know. I mean you're gorgeous but there's so much more to you than your looks that I like. So, I think your plan to distance is the right thing to do before one of us slips up. That being said, know that if you need me for anything, you just have to reach out. You have my number now so if you need me, I'm here. I only want you to be happy, Elle, so you let me know when you truly are, ok?"

He can't see I'm crying because my face is turned towards my window but I suddenly feel the warmth of him as he takes my hand in his. I let out a gasp and he says, "uhhh bless you? Was that a sneeze?" This makes me laugh along with crying as we continue to hold hands. When he pulls up to my house, he turns the car off and we turn to each other to lock eyes. "I don't know how to explain this Elle Green but I feel like I've known you for years." I smile and nod. "I feel the same way, Ryan. Trust me I don't want to leave this car right now, but I know that I have to. Merry Christmas and thank you for tonight." "My pleasure," he says "and Merry Christmas." We both lean in and hug as I take in his scent one last time. Goodbye Ryan I think to myself.

Chapter Twenty-Four

I'm inserting my key in the door when it pushes back a little and I realize Josh is on the other end opening it. I glance over my shoulder and see Ryan has been watching me. He slowly waves to me and then pulls off down the road. It takes everything in me not to have a moment like the end of "The Graduate" and jump in his car leaving my current life and love behind.

Josh looks terrible. Also, incredibly intoxicated. "Where were you?" He demands. "I called you and left you so many messages and you were out with some guy?" I take a seat on the couch and look directly at him. I'm watching him talk but not hearing a word that's coming out of his mouth. Instead, I'm reflecting. This is what he does, what he's always done, turn the blame onto me. Turning something that he did that was terrible and somehow make me feel bad or make me want to apologize. It's classic gaslighting; not only is he not taking responsibility for anything but he's also turning it around to continue the narrative of being the poor victim. Well, I'm not helping him with that storyline anymore. I've got my own story to work on and write. When I see that he's now staring at me and waiting for my response I know this is my chance; whether he's intoxicated or not.

"That MAN", I emphasize, "is not just "some guy". Josh scoffs at this but I continue on. "He is a complete gentleman who was helping me out when my car wouldn't start. He took me to go see my husband for direction and when I encountered my husband was all over another woman, he took me away from the toxic environment and made sure I was ok before bringing me home. Yes, you called me, repeatedly. Which is funny considering when I needed you, you didn't answer, you weren't there. You expect me though to answer you when you realize that you not only screwed up but were caught. No, Josh, I'm not playing things that way anymore. I've completely put myself on the back burner for your needs and your wants; that's not healthy and that's not a two-way street relationship. I've enabled you and that's on me but what isn't on me is the kind of partner you are."

"Ellie, what are you talking about?" He asks as I can see he's starting to get angry. He picks up his beer and chugs it which makes me even more unattracted to him. "I got caught with what? You didn't even let me explain. I have to be nice to people, it's my job. Chelsea is a regular there and yeah, she can be a little flirty but I just play the part. Nothing has happened with her or anyone. I don't get where this is coming from? I'm not a good partner? That's crap! I just went all out for our anniversary and you didn't even seem thankful."

"Josh, let me ask you something", I say calmly. "Why do you think I did not seem thankful? Was it because I didn't hook up with you? See, that's how you associate love and while that's important that's not everything." He goes to interrupt me but I lift my hand up and cut him off. "This may seem out of nowhere but it's probably because I've never vocalized it before. I'm taking ownership of that but what it comes down to is, you can't love me the way I need to be loved. This isn't the best time to have this conversation because you've been drinking but I need some space. Josh, I don't think it's in anyone's benefit if we keep this marriage going. We have great physical chemistry but that's not enough." It's at this moment I see it; Josh's realization that this isn't just a fight. "Wait, what?" He chokes out. "Ellie, you want to leave me?" he asks as his eyes start to water. "What did I do wrong? All I've ever done is love you and I can love you the way you need to be loved; just tell me what to do and I'll do it."

"That's the whole point right there", I say. "I shouldn't have to tell you and you shouldn't have to guess. We both just give out and receive love differently and it's not working for me." He comes over to me on the couch and kneels down so that his hands are on each side of my hips and he's looking into my eyes. "I'm sorry, I just don't feel that way," he says as he grabs my left hand and starts playing with my ring. "I think maybe you need to sleep on it or take a few days and then we can regroup?" When I shake my head no he really lets it out. His head is literally in my lap with tears drenching my pants. I take a step back, figuratively, and look at him and it's like I can see the child version of Josh. The one who really just wants to be accepted and loved but has no clue how to get it. He thinks that he has to keep everyone at arm's length to protect himself but all that does is create more and more space which ends up causing the divide and inevitable ending. He's basically the king of self-sabotaging. I put my arms behind his head and console him while also telling him this is for the best. We stay like this for a while; I haven't even looked at the clock to see what time it is. When he pulls away his eyes are puffy and his face is blotchy and red. I've shed some tears too but for me it feels more cathartic like getting rid of all of the toxicity that happened in the past in this relationship. This feels like a real goodbye; a real closure of what was needed. Even though I had thought I was over what happened years ago, I don't think I really was. This has given me insight into what was really going on in his mind. He was never fighting me; he was fighting himself all along. "So, what do we do?" He asks as he looks up at me with such sadness in his eyes. "Do you leave or do I leave the house?" "I can stay with Gwen," I say. "I just need to call her because my car is still abandoned." "I'll drive you", he announces. "No, you've been drinking a decent amount; give me one second." I take my phone out and text Gwen.

Me- Are you up? I know it's late.

Gwen- Of course, what's up?

Me- Can you come pick me up and can I stay with you for a little while? I know that's a huge ask of you and if you need to ask Greg first, I completely understand.

Gwen- Are you serious? You're staying, end of story. I'll be there in 20 minutes.

"I'm going to go pack up some things", I tell Josh. I can hear him sniffling as I'm loading up my belongings but I know what I've done is the best for both of us. Gwen must have been speeding because I hear the doorbell within minutes. Josh grabs my suitcases and insists on bringing them out to the car. Gwen is making small talk with him which is super awkward but better them than me. After everything is loaded into the car, I turn around and say thank you. "I love you Ellie... Elle", he says. "Even if it's not the way you need to be loved; I love you the only way I know how." "I know," I say as I give him a quick hug. "I know." I get in the car and put my seatbelt on and look over at Gwen. "Alright, I'll wait until we pull out of your driveway but then you need to tell me everything" she says.

Chapter Twenty-Five

I filled Gwen in on everything and it wasn't until three AM that we finally finished talking and fell asleep. The next few days were a blur. Part of me felt I had gone through a breakup (which technically I had, two actually!) And the other part of me felt invigorated. For the first time in my life since my early 20s I was single. Not single in the way that I was on the market and ready to mingle, but single in the way I could direct my life wherever I wanted it to go. It was exhausting always wondering why Josh did something the way he did or wondering when I'd see Ryan and if he'd remember we were married. No, this was now my time! What was I going to do with it? Here's the best part.... I had no idea!

I did things that made me feel alive. I took long walks in the park by Gwen's house, blasting music in my car and singing at the top of my lungs as I took long drives to the beach. I decided where I wanted to eat, if I wanted to eat and what I wanted to eat. No guilt about eating carbs or worrying about how may calories existed in my meals. Instead, I focused on what felt good to my body and what made me feel joy. If I wanted to have a margarita at lunch, I did it! I hadn't realized how my existence had been put on the backburner in a way. With Josh especially but also with Ryan. When he would be away working on the restaurant I would wallow at home. I didn't really go out and do things, explore, see what the world looked like to just me. Even writing my books, I only had done that in my office, in my little space I secluded myself in. I didn't venture out. He had tried to encourage that but I wasn't interested.

Now I made a point to take myself out on weekly road trips. The beach was definitely a favorite of mine but I also loved going to the museum nearby. I loved walking around and spending as much time as I wanted to trying to find the mystery inside of the art. It was beautiful.

I also took up yoga! This was new for me and I was learning so much more than just the poses. I was feeling. When I'd go into my savasana at the end of the class, I'd just sit still letting my mind feel gratitude. Getting a glimpse into who Elle is and just how damn strong she is.

Want to hear something funny? I met Isabelle at one of the classes. Remember Isabelle, I told you about? Well, we got talking about how it was hard for me to get into the pigeon pose which someone ended up with us getting coffee. Our conversation was flowing and it led to talking about our passions, which then of course led me to talking about my book! After she gave me her information and asked me to let her know when I was done with it, I stepped into my car with the biggest smile on my face. I had done this myself. I had made my own connections, which wouldn't have happened if I didn't start getting out of my comfort zone. The universe is funny like that.

Not everything has been sunshine, butterflies and massive growth charts though. I mean I'm not saying it hasn't been hard. It has been. Christmas was especially hard for me. I can't tell you how many times I opened up Ryan's number on my phone wanting desperately to text him.

I even drafted a text to him on Christmas to tell him about my meeting with Isabelle but later decided it was best to leave it be. There was no sense in stirring up emotions on Christmas, no matter how badly I wanted to see him. That honestly wouldn't be fair to him.

SWEET PEAR

I'm not saying that social media stalking was out of the question though. I saw those Christmas photos with him and his family and it just looked so ... lovely. There was a sweet one in particular where his mom was holding the wreath that we made and she looked so happy. I wondered if he thought of me while she was opening it. Did he think of me at all? He looked so cute in the photos where they were all wearing matching pajamas, opening up presents like children again. I used to be part of that group, wearing those matching pjs proudly.

No matter how much I wanted to reach out to him, I knew I couldn't. Josh texted me a lot though. He first texted me saying he missed me. Then he asked me to come home, asked me why this was happening and could he change things? When that didn't work, he went into the past and started sending me inside jokes we had from years ago, pictures of us together in happier times, songs we used to listen to, anything to spark a reaction. I would just double tap and like it as I didn't want it to go into any further communication. It was hard. It was out of my comfort zone. I realized how much of a people pleaser I really had been. I would put aside my desires, my comfort, my thoughts to help others feel better. Gwen and I had many nights playing therapist and patient to self-analyze (with wine) but thank God for those nights. They got me through a lot.

Whenever I felt the urge to call Ryan, I'd make myself write. Even if I felt I had no steam left in me; and it worked. I'm currently halfway through writing my mystery novel! I've kept the same characters' names and their story lines but I've changed how they interact with each other. They're able to have real, honest conversations about how they're feeling while also maintaining a healthy work environment. In some ways it makes the chapters and storyline to me much sexier. There's still tension there but they both know where they stand and really, how refreshing is that?

Today is New Year's Eve and I'm feeling a little down. Ryan and I used to host New Year's Eve at our place. It was always so much fun! He would make all of the appetizers which of course were delicious and I was in charge of the refreshments. I would title the drinks all fun names (I guess I carried that over into this life as well.) and we would all get dressed up and play games. At the end of the night our friends would stay over and it felt like we were back in college. Even though I'm here with Gwen and her family; I still feel a little empty.

I started my day off good though with getting up early, going to a Yoga Class and finishing up a few more chapters of my book at the cute little coffee shop I found. I know it's right next to Sweet Pear but I like the coffee here, ok? I didn't end up seeing Ryan while I was there and I'll admit a piece of me was sad. My plan for tonight is to curl up in my temporary bedroom in comfy clothes and my new best friend, Merlot. He can be a little dry for some but after a few glasses, he gets me laughing. I've decided I'll come out into the family room ten minutes to midnight and celebrate with Gwen and her family. I know this sounds depressing but I honestly am not feeling like socializing this year. I also know that I'll have to start looking for a place. Gwen has told me I could basically move into their in-law suite and as much as I would love that I know it's not my place and I need my own space. I'll start looking in the New Year, I tell myself.

I step into her house when I notice that the kids and Greg aren't sitting in their usual Saturday spots which are on the sofas and that Gwen is in the kitchen pouring two glasses of champagne. "Where's the kids?" I ask her. "Not here" she says as she slowly smiles and opens the fridge. "Where's Greg?" "Not here" she repeats, with her smile growing, opening up the orange juice. "Oh, are they running an errand or something?" "Nope", she beams as pours the tiniest amount into the glasses and brings over the other glass to me. "They're all spending the night at Greg's parents' house." "For New Year's Eve?" I asked. "Yeah, I told Greg that I felt we needed to ring in the New Year, just me and you and he understood. The kids love Greg's parents' place anyways so they'll have a blast." "Gwen" I say sternly, "you didn't have to do that. I don't want to bring you down! You have a family and won't it be weird to celebrate the New Year without them?" "My darling Elle", she says as she places her arm around my shoulder holding up her champagne flute. "You are my family as well. I want nothing more than to celebrate it with you.

Also, might I remind you I am childless and husbandless? Let's make the most of this fun night! Cheers" she says as she clinks her glass with mine. "I love you!" I cry out as I give her a hug while trying not to spill my mimosa. "I love you too, now let's find something for you to wear because we're going out!

Chapter Twenty-Six

One great thing about Gwen is she has the best clothes and ironically, we are about the same size. I'm jumping up while zippering the fake black leather pants I'm borrowing as she's picking out statement earrings for me to wear. "Hmm", she says as she looks me over. "You're going to need red lipstick." "Why would I need red.... Wait a minute; are you setting me up?" "No, but look, people hookup on New Year's Eve, right? It happens. That's what you need in the worst way right now." "No, no" I shake my head. "I don't need that and I don't want that. I can't even picture looking at another man right now. I'm over relationships." "Uh huh" she says as she's pouring more champagne in her glass and then topping mine off as well. "Yeah, you say that but then you're gonna lock eyes with a dreamy McDreamboat and you're going to be like, I said what now? Look, I won't pressure you; if it happens it happens but there's no harm in looking hot is there? No offense Elle, but you've been looking a little frumpy lately." "Frumpy?" I whisper. "Well, I don't want that. Alright Gwen, give me a Sandra Dee makeover."

I take a look at myself in the mirror and dang, she did good! I look great; I mean really great. I have a glow on my face that I thought you could only get when you were pregnant. I'm puffing out my curled hair with my fingers giving it the last bit of volume it needs and smiling in the mirror to make sure I don't have any red lipstick on my teeth when I hear Gwen shout out yes in the other room. "What?" I ask. "Oh, we just got an invite," she says as she dances back into the bathroom. "An invite? To where?" "To Liv's" she sings out. "I totally forgot she was having a New Year's Eve party on the rooftop. She told me about it months ago but I must have blocked it out, Oh Elle... the stars are aligning for us!" Ok, now I'm excited. Liv's parties are seriously the best. The best food, the best decor, the best locations. I'm pretty sure she saves up for them starting January 2nd of the year prior. There's a guest list and everything; I mean she goes all out. "The stars do seem to be aligning", I say as I pucker my lips onto a tissue. "Tonight is going to be one for the books; I can feel it."

I'm scrolling through social media and posting selfies of Gwen and I in our car when we pull up to the party. "Oh my gosh, she has a doorman?" I ask. "He has a clipboard; how much did she pay for this?" "Who cares?" Gwen says. "We are on the list and that's all that matters, let's go!" "Hang on", I say as I notice something on my phone. A picture was just posted from a party that Josh's tagged in. It's at the bar and looks like they're having a Pre-NYE party and there he is. He's got a top hat on and a noisemaker in his mouth and next to him with her arm around his waist is none other than Chelsea. I show the phone to Gwen and she takes a minute to process and says, "Wait a minute, is that that girl?" "It is", I say. "I have good news though; I don't feel upset. I don't feel anything really. Not in a numb way but in a hey, if she makes him happy then I wish them the best kind of feeling." "I think that's great then" Gwen says. "It shows you really have moved on and are in a healthy place. So, let's take that healthy place booty and get up so we can shake it", she laughs as she grabs my hand and leads me out of the door.

After confirming our name on the list, which by the way, is a wonderful feeling that will never get old; we arrive. The elevator opens and brings us into the main lounge. Wow is all I can say as

I scan around the room. This is better than anything I could have ever imagined! It's absolutely beautiful. There are ice sculptures, people walking around with trays of hor d'oeuvres and champagne flutes. The place is filled but not in a claustrophobic crowded kind of way. You can walk with ease around people without feeling like you're pushing people out of the way but it's also not too sparse where you stand around awkwardly trying to blend in either. In a word, it's just perfect.

Liv spots us from across the room and screams. We echo her scream and run to each other into a cozy triangular hug of love. "Gwen I'm so glad you're here and Elle, ok bombshell, divorce looks good on you!" I look at her and see a moment of panic on her face as she darts her eyes quickly to Gwen and back to me. I start laughing and it breaks all three of us out into laughter. "So, you're ok then?" She asks me with genuine concern. "I really am, Liv." I say. "I think this was a long time coming actually. I have never felt so at ease with myself as I do right now." "Well, yay I've got my single girl back" she says as she puts her arm around me. "Ok, so since I've been single since, like birth, I make it a point to invite only the most handsome single men ever to my parties so you're in luck. I have so many bachelors to introduce you to!" "We're not pressuring her", Gwen says. "I already got the talk from her earlier." "Oh... ok so we're pretending you're not going to hook up with anyone tonight, ok got it", Liv says as she winks at me and is suddenly whisked away from one of the handsome bachelors she mentioned. "Alright, let's get this started" I smile to Gwen as we each grab a flute and cheers.

You know how when you're having so much fun it feels like you've entered a different vortex? Like where time doesn't exist while hours fly by and you are at a perfect blend of tipsy but not overly buzzed? That's exactly how this night is going. I look at my phone and see it's nine o'clock already. I also see I have a text from Josh which I decide to promptly delete before fully reading it. All I saw was, "Ellie, I miss my..." I'll think he was saying, Ellie, I miss my deodorant. Gosh, I smell! That thought makes me giggle a little to myself and I start to think maybe I should eat a little something so that I can keep this tipsy before drunk feeling going. I walk over to one of the waiters holding the hor d'oeuvres tray and ask them what it is. "Oh, this is a goat cheese toast topped with mission figs and drizzled with a balsamic glaze," he says as he hands me one with a tiny napkin. "A goat cheese" I start to repeat as I hear a voice interrupt with the word "Elle?" coming from behind me.

I turn around and see it's Ryan, looking so hot in his chef's uniform. "Ryan, what are you doing here," I ask. "I, um... I'm, my restaurant is catering this party, you look gorgeous" he stutters out all in one sentence. "I mean, wow... You're...wow." I feel my cheeks flush as I look down unable to hide my smile. "Thank you", I say with a quiet laugh. "I'm sorry, that was inappropriate", he says. "I don't know why I can't seem to censor myself around you. Like that, I shouldn't have just said that; I could have just thought that. Alright, I'm done talking", he laughs.

"No, I love that about you," I say. "I've always thought censoring yourself is overrated anyways. Why not put it all out there, you know?" "Yeah" he says as I watch him quickly scan me up and down and now it's his turn to have flushed cheeks. "It feels like it's been a while since I've seen you Elle, how are you?" "I'm really great", I answer truthfully. "I've been living with Gwen for a little while now actually; going through a divorce." "Oh", he says as he pauses. "Are you, are you doing ok with that?" He asks hesitantly. "That's a lot." "I am, I really am. I told you I knew it should've happened a while ago, I just didn't realize how much he held me back, until I met you really. See, no filter either", I laugh as I tap his arm. "So, how are you?" "Oh, I'm good", he says after a stunned beat. "Work has been very busy which is great.

Oh, my mom loved the gift by the way! I was going to message you on Christmas to tell you that and to wish you a Merry Christmas too but it didn't feel..." "Like the right time?" I answer for him. "Yeah, the right time," he says back. "Look, I know we said we shouldn't be friends but, I think about you a lot, Elle. I miss your company." "I do too", I say a little too fast but without embarrassment this time. "I miss you so much; can we hang out?" "Hang out?" He laughs. "Sure, we can hang out. I have to get back to work but, maybe I'll see you when I'm cleaning up after? If you're still around?" "I'll be sure to be here", I reply back. "See you soon Ryan", I say as I walk away. Gwen is staring at me with the biggest smile on her face.

"I thought you said you weren't into men right now. I thought you said you couldn't even picture talking to a guy" she's saying as she's in my face teasing me. "I thought you said you weren't going to have a hookup." "I did", I say back with a smirk. "He's not just any guy though and trust me, I want a whole lot more than just a hook up with him."

Chapter Twenty-Seven

I keep looking over at the door to where the kitchen is. Where he is. I know tonight is supposed to be about me and my independence and it is, but I'm also hyperly aware of his presence. I can smell him, feel him, taste him. It's like I'm having an animalistic attraction and I want nothing more than to pounce. Pull it together girl, I think to myself. That's not what your relationship with Ryan is like. It's true; partly. It used to feel like that, feel like electricity was shooting through my body. From the first moment we touched fingers when I gave him my phone number at the restaurant but then as time went on the electricity started to diminish. Resentment started to build as I felt he was spending more and more time at work and less and less time with me. I had my writing and that kept me busy but I still felt an uneasiness of being alone. I don't know what the fear was.

Was it that I thought if he wasn't physically near me that meant he also wasn't mentally near me and therefore would leave me? Was I resentful of the fact that he spent so much time at work trying to create his new baby that he wouldn't have time or energy for me? "What the hell, Elle?" I say under my breath. I realize now what I was doing. I was projecting all of my insecurities; all of my old patterns and old cycles from past relationships and past outcomes onto him. Even though I was pouring my words and thoughts into my books, I was still losing a huge part of myself and putting it onto Ryan's shoulders. That's a lot to put onto someone. I wonder if he felt it. I wonder if that might have been part of the reason he liked to get away from our house and get away from that energy. Maybe it was suffocating to him.

It makes sense when I would allow myself to indulge fantasies of better times, I would go back to Josh. Why wouldn't I? That was the part that I was missing in my marriage with Ryan. The physical part that used to be there but left before I even realized it. It was too hard to remember and fantasize about our times together, it would just make me sad. I could, though, go back to Josh. That relationship had ended so it would be easier to replay those moments. It was "safe". Of course, the universe would mistaken that energy and form it into us running into each other again. Of course, it would test me to see what it was I really wanted. Of course, I would fail.

Did I fail? Something happened to me this time around. It's like an interrogation light is now shining on me. I can almost feel the heat on my neck and see the blinding rays of artificial light. This was never about Ryan or Josh or Hunter, my first boyfriend in high school, for that matter. This was always about me. Always about what made me.... me, without someone else. What were my needs, my wants, my desires and how do they change with time and also when I'm feeling at ease and comfort? I think I mistook comfort as boredom. My mind is spinning and I feel like I can almost hear the pop of my bubble as I'm slowly brought back into reality.

My first reaction is to find Gwen immediately and tell her everything, but I don't. This is for me; this is my reminder. I am perfect and whole as is. Everyone and everything I choose in my life is a wonderful addition. I imagine how I must look to anyone watching me right now. I'm sure I look crazed, or drunk with a big smile on my face but I don't care. I walk over to Gwen and Liv and give them each a hug. "Yes, Elle's drunk!!" Liz yells. "No, I'm not actually", I say. "I just wanted to hug you because I love you and I'm so glad to have you in my life." Gwen looks at me and I see her squinting her eyes trying to analyze what's just happened. "Hmmm... looks like you had a profound moment there" she says. "I did, I smile. I really did."

"This is such a great way to ring in the New Year", I yell to Gwen. "What?" She yells back as we are both now jumping up and down dancing to Prince's 1999, always a classic. "This is a great way to start the Year" I yell again. "What about new beer?" She asks. "Oh my god", I yell back. "This is great!!" She smiles and then belts out, "tonight I'm gonna party" ... Someone is passing out New Years' leis, which I'm not totally sure why because nothing else in this party is Hawaiian theme but I'm not going to argue about it as I let them slide the black and silver lei over my neck. Gwen and I are grabbing two more drinks when two guys come over to us. "Hey there pretty ladies" the one guy slurs out; "I'm Randy" "Hey Man", Gwen says, "nice hat!" "You wanna wear it?" He asks. "You can totally wear it." "Sure", she shrugs as he puts the hat on her head. His friend looks much less intoxicated and is super cute. "Hi, I'm Elle," I say, putting my hand out to shake. "Elle, that's a really pretty name," he says. "I'm Brandon. We couldn't help noticing you both having such a great time dancing." "Yeah, it's hot!!" Randy yells out again. "Sorry, my friend is really drunk," Brandon says as he steps in closer to me. "I mean, if there's any time to let loose, I'm pretty sure today is the day" I say back with a laugh. "You girls want to go back to our place", Randy asks. "Married", Gwen says while holding up her hand to show off her ring. "What about you?" Brandon asks me. I take a second to look at him. He's very cute. He has light green eyes with almost a mix of gold in them. Honestly, he looks fun, and respectable but I know in my heart it wouldn't be right. "I'm not married anymore, but I'm going to have to pass. I'm having a great time with my girlfriend right now. Nice to meet both of you though." We promptly turn around and walk away. "Really, Elle? He was so cute." "He was", I say "but you're cuter."

Chapter Twenty-Eight

It's about ten minutes to midnight and you can feel the collective energy light up. Everyone is smiling and laughing. Some people are dripping sweat from dancing and some are in the corner looking like they might need to get some air outside. I'm currently looking over my shoulder, watching Ryan. He's talking and laughing with his employees and I'm literally falling in love with him all over again. I forgot how sociable he is. Everyone really does take to him instantly and enjoy talking with him. I mean, you could sit him next to a wall and he'd come back and tell you all about the wall's back story along with a list of its likes and dislikes. What am I doing? I'm standing here like a creeper watching him. What's going to happen after it hits midnight? Are we going to have a meaningful conversation? Are we going to hook up? Are we going to end up together? Am I ready for that? Do I deserve that? He said he thinks about me. He wants me as much as I want him, I know it. My palms are sweating and I can feel my heart pumping. Gwen's been talking about this recipe she wants to make for us for New Year's tomorrow, but I can't concentrate. I shouldn't be watching him like this. I shouldn't be fantasizing about what our future will look like. I should take this cautiously; move very slowly.

It's the right thing to do. "What's happening?" Gwen asks me as she notices something is coming over me. I look over at her and am unable to speak. It's like I'm moving in slow motion. I hand her my glass, turn around and start walking.

The music has blurred together and I no longer hear words but hear the beats, feel the beats. Is this my heart beating? I don't know but I'm now moving fast. I'm putting my hand on people's shoulders to get past them, not even saying sorry or excuse me. I'm making my way closer and closer. He doesn't notice me coming at first but I see him look over as I'm a few feet away. I don't stop to say hi, I don't stop to wait until his conversation is over. He's pulled back from talking with his employees and I see their eyes trail to where he's looking as well. "Hey", he manages to get out as I'm already pulling the Lei off of my neck and standing on my tippy toes to put it over his head. In one swift motion I get it on and grab the front to pull it towards me. He leans down and I see a mixture of shock and longing in his eyes. I don't think, I just bring him towards me to have our lips meet each other.

This is the best kiss I've ever had in my life. I'm serious, better than my wedding day, better than our honeymoon, better than anyone from my past. We are so enveloped in each other that I don't even notice people are now starting to countdown to midnight. We pull away and he takes a deep breath. "Elle", he says to me as he looks at me like I'm the most beautiful thing he's ever laid eyes on. "I've been wanting to do that for a while now. I wanted to be respectful though, are you sure?" "I'm more than sure", I say," and I'm sure I want to do it again." I put my hand around his neck as he leans down into me with such care. We continue kissing, in between laughing and then when it hits midnight and everyone is cheering and blowing noisemakers, we are tightly hugging each other, slightly swaying back and forth.

I don't want this feeling to end, and then I realize, it doesn't have to. People are starting to leave the party and I'm slowly becoming aware again of the outside world. The beats are morphing now into lyrics and I'm able to make out the song, "Closing Time" is playing, signaling the party is in fact closing out. I look up at Ryan and see he looks to be at complete ease. There's no worry or confusion in his eyes, but instead they're filled with happiness and love. I know what that face looks like, I've seen it many times before. "I can't stop smiling", I say with the cheesiest grin. "I know me either", he says back. "I do have to get my team squared away though so they can clean up and leave but are you going to be here for a little while longer? I'd love to hang out, maybe have a proper drink with you now that I'm off the clock?" "I'd love that", I say "and don't worry, I know the host so I'll make sure the drinks are flowing." "Ok good", he says. "I'll be right back then." He turns around and I watch him walk away and see him turn his head back to look at me once more. When he realizes I haven't moved I hear him say under his breath, "Oh hell!" as he comes walking back to where I'm standing.

"What are you doing to me, Miss Green?" he asks as he lifts me up and lays another kiss on me. "I should ask what you're doing to me Mr. Elverson because I literally can't move." "Well, you have to", he laughs "or I won't be able to either. I'll just keep picturing you standing here looking all drop dead gorgeous and all I want to do is … no, I'm going to censor myself this time", he says with a devious smile. I feel warmth go from my heart all the way down to my feet and I've never been more attracted to someone. "You can censor your words", I say playfully, "but you can't censor your body language." He raises his eyebrows and I know he feels what I'm feeling. "Alright, I know you've got work to do so I'm going to turn myself around and walk away, for real this time." I do as I say as I feel his eyes on my back. I sing under my breath the part of the song that I've never identified with more than before, "I know who I want to take me home."

Chapter Twenty-Nine

It's a little after one AM and there's a few of us stragglers left. Our shoes are off, we're sitting on the floor against the wall with our legs crossed polishing off the last of the hors d'oeuvres. I mean, we each have a tray perched on our laps like they're TV dinners. Liv is in the corner making out with ironically the guy Brandon who offered to bring me to his home earlier. Aw, I think to myself with a smile, good for them. Maybe one day we'll be guests at their wedding! Brandon's friend is passed out on a chair on the other side of the room with his hands placed perfectly across his lap. Gwen is asking me for the fifth time to tell her what happened with Ryan and I. "Tell me again", she sings as she hands me a coconut shrimp. "Ok", I say as I quickly eat the shrimp. "So, I don't know what happened, it's like someone turned a button on inside me and I was programmed to walk over to him and kiss him. I couldn't help myself."

"I'm glad you couldn't", I hear him say behind me. I turn around and laugh. "Of course, out of all the moments, you come over during that part." "Yeah, it's a skill I have", he laughs back as he slumps down and sits next to me. He puts his arm around my waist and brings me close and I feel like I'm in high school all over again. Just the slightest touch of his body next to mine gets me going.

Gwen pours a glass of champagne and passes it over to Ryan. "Here you go, sir. You deserve this especially after feeding us crazies the whole night." "Well, thank you," he says as he smiles and shows off that dimple I love so much.

"So", Gwen says, then pauses. Oh no, I know that pause. That's when Gwen knows she shouldn't ask what she really wants to but she does anyways. So, she starts up again. "What's next now? For you two", she motions as she moves onto eating cold risotto balls. I look over at Ryan and don't see any nervousness in his eyes. I know he's just as happy as I am right now. "What's next is whatever we want." I say as I grab his hand and interlock our fingers. "I like that", he says. "Although, I would like to take you out on a real date. I feel like the last time we were together, well, that wasn't really a date. Although there were moments it felt real. Until, ya know you told me you couldn't see me anymore on the way home." There's a brief moment of silence and awkwardness. Shoot, I thought this would be easier. I thought we could blow past that as if it didn't happen and instead be happy we are finally able to be together. That's not how life works though, I should know that. "You're right", I say back to him. "You didn't deserve that but I was doing what I thought was best for both of us. I knew I had to completely end things with Josh before acting on what I so badly wanted to act on." I squeeze his hand slightly and he squeezes it back telling me everything. We want each other. Now. Gwen seems to pick up on the tension and mumbles something and leaves as fast as her legs can take her. We then spend the next twenty or so minutes doing what "high schoolers" in love do. Make out without caring who sees us.

When I'm finally able to pull myself apart from his face, I realize I am exhausted. His lips are smeared with my red lipstick and my lips feel chapped but also are buzzing like I just applied a cool mint chap stick over them. "You look tired", he smiles. "I am", I say as I wipe the lipstick residue off of his face. "I really don't want to be. I want to keep doing this, and more all night long." "As much as I want that too", he says, "I also want it to be when we aren't struggling to keep our eyes open. How about we take the night to rest and reset and I'll call you tomorrow to see if you want to go out? Unless you have plans, you probably have plans." "I have breakfast plans with Gwen but give me a call and we can figure out times tomorrow." I look over and see Gwen is pouring the last of the champagne into her flute but decides against that and instead puts the bottle to her lips. "Your friend is fun", he says. "She is", I say as I put my head against his chest hearing his heartbeat, "she's the best."

Gwen and I are now back at her house sitting on her bed curled up in blankets. "Gwen, I have a problem," I announce. "How?" She laughs. "How could you possibly have a problem? You kissed Ryan tonight! Finally, this is what you've been wanting all along." "I know, I know but I still feel guilty for what I did to Ryan. I know he doesn't know what happened or even remember us being married but I do. I betrayed him and I feel like I should tell him." Gwen smacks my arm. "Ow, what? Is that so terrible to feel?" I ask her. "Yes, you're talking crazy Elle", she yells in my face as she throws a pillow at my head. "You've been given a second chance; don't you see that? You can rewrite your history with Ryan. Tomorrow you are going to go on a romantic date and then you're going to have an amazing night, like it's the first time. Don't muddle that up with guilt on something that none of us have seen or know of, except you."

I know she's right but I just can't shake the feeling. It feels deceitful, even if it was in a different life. I lay my head on the pillow pondering about my next move when I drift off to sleep.

Chapter Thirty

I wake up the next morning feeling slightly hungover and confused until I realize today is the day. I'm going on a date with Ryan! I turn over with such excitement I accidentally elbow Gwen in the face. "Sorry", I whisper. "It's fine," she growls. "I need coffee." "Me too", I say. "Hey, instead of cooking breakfast, why don't we go to that cute little coffee shop I've been going to recently." "The one by Sweet Pear?" She asks while stretching. "I guess your guilt has subsided?" "It's still there, but excitement is coming at the forefront instead." "Good", she says. "That's how it should be. Alright, five more minutes and then we'll get up."

We are sitting in the coffee shop devouring French toast, fresh fruit and eggs benedict and I feel like I've entered heaven. Whenever Gwen and I go out we always order way too much food and then have it spread across the table like a buffet. It's really the only way to eat if I'm being honest. I'm sipping my cinnamon latte when I glance out the window and see Ryan walk by. "Ahhh" I scream out as I knock on the window. "Oh, girl you got it bad", Gwen laughs. He looks over and I see his eyes sparkle as he recognizes it's me. A smile forms on his lips and it takes everything in me not to jump on him. Ah, screw it, I'm doing it.

I quickly get up out of my chair and run outside as I hear Gwen giggling behind me. The cold air and wind greet me instantly as I open the door and I realize I forgot my jacket. "Hiiii", I chatter out to him. "Elle, you must be freezing," he says as he takes me in a warm hug. "Just a little cold", I say as I inhale a hint of his cologne ... "Alright look I tried to play it cool in there but I can't hide it well. I'm just drawn to you", I confess to him. He gives a surprised laugh and says, "well the feeling is absolutely mutual Miss Green." He leans down and tilts my chin up to give me the sweetest kiss. The warmth of his lips makes me instantly melt.

"You look cute today too. How do you not look hungover?" he asks. "Oh well see I'm what people would call a hangover expert at this point of my life. I've learned that a huge breakfast with lots of calories tends to bring life back into me. Where are you off to?" I ask. His expression reads amusement towards me. "I'm heading into the restaurant to get things setup for the lunch shift. I was going to call you in a little bit but since you're here I guess I can ask you now. You want to grab dinner around seven?" "Sure", I beam. "Do you want to meet somewhere or are you going to be picking me up?" "Is that even a question?" he laughs. "I'll pick you up, you just have to give me Gwen's address." "Ok, I'll text that to you then because I'm turning into Frosty the snowman right now, so I gotta get back inside." "Yes, go inside and defrost and we can warm up later" he says as he gives me a little wink. "Oh, I can't wait, believe me" I say as I grab a hold of the collar of his jacket and bring him to me. I make sure to kiss him in a way that will make him want more. As I pull away, I can see in his eyes that it's worked. Ryan clears his throat. "Well, alright that's one way to start the morning. Text me the info. and I'll see you at seven." "Alright, see you later" I chatter out as I run back inside the coffee shop and plop back down in front of Gwen. She's looking at me with the biggest smile on her face. "What?" I ask, trying to hide my grin. "I feel like we should go shopping", she says as she sits back in the booth. "For like the dirtiest lingerie possible because I can already see how this night is going to go down."

"Noooo" I say with a smile looking down at my latte. "I mean, yes I want that trust me but not for the first date. I don't want to cloud anything either; because I know how that can get in the middle of things." "Yeah but, Elle, technically you've done this before with Ryan. I mean, he doesn't know that but I mean don't you feel like you've waited long enough?" "Yes, I do" I say "but this is new for him. I want to move at his pace." "Ok", Gwen says as she pops a strawberry in her mouth. "Still, no harm in shopping, right?" "Uhm ... there's never any harm in shopping," I reply with a smile on my face I just can't seem to erase, no matter how hard I try.

I'm so excited imaging how our night is going to go. It really feels like a clean slate and I'm looking at Ryan through fresh eyes again. I'm getting a glimpse back into how he was at the beginning of our relationship, but even more so. He's different. I'm different too, I suppose. Maybe this twisted reality happened so that we could meet again when the timing was right? When he was able to live out his passion without me in the equation and eliminating all of the beginning of opening a business stress onto our relationship?

I'm also feeling a little nervous; like butterflies in my belly kind of emotions. I used to dread going on dates back in the day. I remembered I'd get such bad anxiety that I even cancelled some. It was almost easier for me to kiss a random guy in a bar then go on an actual date. I'm sure that probably has something to do with vulnerability and feelings if I really took time to delve into it. With Ryan though, I cannot wait for this date. I cannot wait to kiss him again, smell him, watch the wrinkles form on the sides of his eyes when he's excited. Just thinking about hearing his voice is almost too much for me to handle. I need to relax my mind and enjoy this time.

Gwen and I did in fact go shopping and I didn't necessarily buy lingerie but I did buy a new sexy lacey bra and matching underwear. I mean, you never know what's going to happen and you might as well be prepared, right?

When we walked into the house after lunchtime, I think our hangovers started to kick in giving us a delayed reaction. "Gwen, I'm hitting a wall," I said as I collapsed onto the couch and took my shoes off. I stretched my body out and Gwen threw a blanket over to me that landed right on my face. "Here you go girl. I think we should take a little cat nap. I'll set my alarm for an hour and then when we wake up, we'll get ourselves hydrated and ready. You need to be bright eyed and bushy tailed for this date. Damn, I feel like I'm living through you right now!" I laid the blanket over my body and curled into the couch, molding myself as if I were now a part of it. "Yeah," I replied back. "That's a good idea. I really do need to shut my mind off for a minute. You're not living through me; you have a beautiful life, Gwen! I'm just trying to get mine back." When I heard silence, I looked over my shoulder and saw she was fast asleep on the loveseat. A little smirk formed on my mouth and before I knew it, I too was off to la la land.

We woke up slowly and a little later than we wanted too but but within an hour we were back to feeling like ourselves. The time is now a little before five o'clock and I'm taking a bubble bath when I hear my phone ring in the other room. "Elle, Ryan's calling you!" Gwen shouts. "Shoot, I'm in the bath, ummm Gwen can you answer it?" "Hello" ... I hear Gwen purr out. "No this is Gwen; Elle is indisposed at the moment. She's currently taking a luxurious bubble bath getting all pretty for your date tonight." "Gwen! "I yell out with embarrassment. She opens the door while holding my phone up to her ear and gives me a thumbs up signal. "Ohhh" she giggles as she throws back her head. "Haha yeah that's so true!" "What's so true?" I ask. "What?" She says, "oh hang on a second Ryan." "I'm on the phone, Elle", she laughs. I give her a don't mess with me look and she quickly puts Ryan on speakerphone. "Hey Ryan", I giggle. "I have you on speakerphone by the way." "Oh, ok hey Elle" he laughs back. "Sorry to disrupt your bath time but I wanted to run something by you before you start getting ready."

My stomach drops. It's now that I start to get nervous.

"Sure, go ahead," I say trying to sound like I'm floating in nothing but calm vibes over here. "Alright so, we could get all dressed up and go out to a fancy restaurant and that would be great and all but I was thinking it could also be nice if I picked you up and made you dinner here at my house. I know you had to get all dressed up yesterday so maybe it would be nice to just dress in comfortable clothes and relax while I cook for you. What do you think?" "Honestly? I think that sounds absolutely amazing and just what I need actually" I say as I put some bubbles in my hand and slowly blow on them. "Only thing I want to change to that plan is I'll drive to you. There's no sense in you picking me up to drive me back to where you started." "Are you sure", he asks. "I really don't mind at all. I'm sure", I say with a smile. "Just text me your address and I'll be there by seven." We say goodbye and I'm glad he hangs up first so I don't have to get out of the bath or yell for Gwen to come in and end the call for me. I stare at the phone that was just housing his voice and just like that, my nerves have vanished. I place the silky bubbles on my body and admire the way they look on my skin. I feel completely blissful in this moment and let out a squeal of delight before slipping under the warm water.

Chapter Thirty-One

I have to say, this is the most comfortable and confident I've ever felt going on a date. True, I've had my first date already with Ryan but this is different. You see, on our first date we actually did dress up and go out to a fancy restaurant and it was amazing. This though feels more like me. The me that has on my most comfortable skinny jeans, white sleeveless bodysuit layered with my oversized olive cardigan and completed with white Adidas sneakers. I applied light makeup on my face and my hair was half blow dried letting the rest air dry naturally; showcasing my actual wavy hair. Pulling into Ryan's driveway I can't help but gasp as I see his house come into view. It is everything I've ever wanted and dreamed of. It looks warm and inviting and also impressive. I wonder if he hired someone to decorate because although he has decent taste it's nothing like this.

As I head up his walkway, I can hear the faint sound of music playing inside. I ring the doorbell and hear his footsteps coming closer to the door and there it is. The electricity feeling is already happening before I even saw him. Just knowing his body is on the other side of the door waiting for my body to enter is starting to make me warm all over. He opens the door and it literally takes my breath away. My God, he is just so handsome. He's wearing dark washed jeans that just happen to fit perfectly and a button down light blue collared shirt with the sleeves rolled up. He has a few of the top buttons unbuttoned and my eyes immediately go to that space where his skin is exposed. "Hey there cutie, get in here," he smiles as he grabs my hand and leads me inside.

I let him take my purse and all of my senses are immediately heightened. I hear 50's soulful music playing in the room next to us on an actual record player; it has the crackly sounds and everything. I feel and see immediately there's a fireplace in his living room and I can smell something delicious coming from the kitchen. "Is this a joke?" I laugh out loud. "What do you mean?" he asks with slight concern. "I mean, this is your house? This house is gorgeous! Not that I didn't think you'd live in a beautiful environment. It's just, I didn't expect, this," I say as I dramatically place my arms out to encompass everything I'm viewing. "I mean, this is like my dream house ... sorry if that sounded weird." He laughs then. "No, it doesn't, but I appreciate the compliment. It happens to be my dream home as well.

To be honest, I wouldn't have been able to pull this all together if it wasn't for my employees forcing me to hire an interior decorator. I always thought that kind of stuff was silly but once I started explaining what things I liked and the vibe I wanted, it was really cool to see it all come together. Would you like a glass of wine? I have a bottle of red I'm about to open", he says as he turns around to grab the wine opener. "Sure, I'd love a glass," I say. My head is swirling. I feel like Ryan has come so far in this lifetime. Was it me that held him back, I wonder? I just can't picture him working with an interior designer and the fact that his house and space looks and feels like what I've always dreamed of and wanted isn't lost on me either.

I follow him into the kitchen and almost pass out. It's spectacular. This is absolutely a chef's kitchen. It's huge and sitting in the middle is a huge dark wooden island and the lighting above is magnificent. I see he has a beautiful rustic looking sign on his wall that displays the words, "Sweet Pear". He opens the bottle and starts pouring the wine into an oversized stemmed glass and it's at this moment that I really see how successful he is. I take a seat at one of the gray upholstered barstool chairs and try to hide the look of shock on my face. "Elle, are you ok?", he asks me. "You look like you could get sick." "I'm sorry, I'm trying not to freak out. Your house is just so beautiful and you are such a humble person. I hope you know how amazing you are, like this is so, so impressive. I'm proud of you and all that you've accomplished." "Well, thank you," he says while he takes a sip of his wine. I see his dimple appear and it makes me smile.

"You really know how to give a guy a compliment and make him feel good. I mean, people say nice things but I don't know, for some reason when you do, I really feel it." "Well, I really mean it," I say back. "I'm not saying other people don't but I mean, I really do feel it." I take a moment before I say what's also on my mind. "It's just, you have all of this and I don't know, I hope you're not disappointed I don't have all of that to offer." Damn this conversation got deep quickly, I think. "Why would you disappoint me?" he asks. "Yes, this is all nice and my restaurants do really well, but it's just things Elle. I don't base your value as a person on anything but you being yourself", he says with a smile. I stare at him in amazement and we lock eyes for what feels like hours. It takes everything in me to look away first and change the subject so I don't do what it is I really want to do.

"So, um what's on the menu?" I ask, changing the topic. "Well," he clears his throat, "it's a very complicated, very fancy recipe of fettuccine and homemade meatballs with my famous pasta sauce. I remember you said before that you really liked pasta so I figured, well this goes with the whole cozy/ comfort theme." "It also goes well with red wine," I say as I hold up my glass. "Oh, wait … that's a good idea," he says as he comes around the side of the island to stand next to me. I catch another whiff of his cologne and it immediately sends a message to my brain to kiss him. Not yet Elle, I think. You need to remain strong and hold out for a little while longer.

"Let's make a toast and cheers", he announces. "Ok, what shall we cheers to" I ask. "Hmm…", he takes a moment to think and I am staring at his face just simply admiring everything I see. The way his brows furrow when he's deep in thought. The moment that he realizes what he wants to say and how his eyes glisten when he's come to that moment; I know this man down to my core. I love this man.

"Ok, I got it", he says with a big smile. "Miss Green, can you please raise your glass?" I do as I'm told. "Alright, I'd like to cheers to the beginning. This is our first date and I feel like I've been waiting a long time for this day. I can't wait to continue getting to know you and so, yeah, I'd like to cheers to the beginning of getting to know each other. Is that corny?" "No", I say as I discreetly wipe away a tear that's begun to form. "That is absolutely the perfect toast. Cheers", I say as I clink glasses with him and as we both take a sip, I think in my head how lucky I really am to have this new beginning with him. The wine goes down so smoothly and has hints of an oaky aftertaste which is my favorite. This date feels like a freaking dream. Am I still asleep on Gwen's couch? I pinch my arm quickly while he's taking a sip and it instantly hurts. Ok, nope ... not a dream, I tell myself.

"Alright, so wait until you try this sauce", he says smoothly as he's back at the large stainless-steel pot stirring with a wooden spoon. "Come around to me" he directs. I listen to his command so fast that I almost trip over my feet. He picks the spoon up with one hand and is cupping underneath it with the other so it doesn't spill. "Ok, let me know what you think", he says as he's bringing the spoon closer to my mouth. I place my glass of wine down on the island and lightly blow on the sauce. When I look up over my lashes slowly into his eyes; I see a mix of intrigue and lust looking back at me. I have a quick moment where I envision myself pushing the spoon away and jumping up to him instead, wrapping my legs around his hips as he leads me to the bedroom while kissing my neck and tearing off my clothes.

Snap out of it Elle, I tell myself internally. It's too late. I can feel the redness rising and taking over my cheeks as I notice a little smile starts to form on the corners of his lips. It's like he's living in my head and can hear my thoughts.

I bring my mouth closer to the tip of the spoon and the most delectable flavors surround my tastebuds. "Oh my God", I say as I wipe the sauce that has made its way to the corner of my mouth. "What is in this, crack? This is seriously delicious!" "Great", he says with a big smile. "That's exactly the reaction I was hoping for." "No, but what's really in it? ", I ask. "Oh, I can't tell you that", he says playfully. "A good chef never reveals his secrets."

"Please" I plead as I pout my bottom lip out. "Oh man", he says. "You keep doing that and we're both in trouble". "How so", I question seductively. "Oh, I think you know how so", he says in a deep, husky voice as he's stirring the sauce. He pauses and then looks over at me with desire in his eyes. I feel the temperature rise in me like mercury in a thermometer. He then turns to face me, leans down and kisses my pouted lips. It starts out as a quick, soft kiss but as he pulls back, I see something change in his eyes.

He puts down the spoon and places his hands on each side of my neck. His fingers are touching the bottoms of my ear lobes and his mouth meets mine again with a hard kiss. Cue the make out session. It needed to happen. I can't help myself and I do in fact jump up to him wrapping my legs around his waist. His hands travel down to my butt as he grabs my cheeks to lift me up onto the island so that we are now at eye level. This is seriously, seriously hot, I think to myself. I tightly wrap my legs around him and place my hand around his neck, wrapping my fingers into his hair. We take moments in between kissing telling each other how much we want one another and then he suddenly pulls back and stops it.

"Alright, don't laugh at me Elle", he says in between heavy breaths, "but I want this to be special. Not that it wouldn't be spectacular if it went further. I mean, I could take you right now into my bedroom" he says as he glances down to the area, I assume is his bedroom and then his eyes meet mine again. Oh man, there goes that zinging feeling buzzing all over my body. I've missed this feeling. I've especially missed this feeling with Ryan, my husband. I honestly didn't know if I could ever feel it again in the past life we shared, but here I am recharged and ready to go. "The thing is though Elle", he continues, "I've always rushed things in the past and I don't want to do that with you. I want to take my time with you. Is that ok?" he asks as he's got his hands on each side of my face running his fingers through my hair slowly. It's incredibly seductive. I turn to my right and give his hand a light kiss and then look at him directly. I'm quite hyped up right now so I have to take a minute to calm down. After taking a few breaths I'm able to begin speaking. "I understand what you're saying and I honestly have never had a guy tell me that. It's always been quick moving for me as well and as foreign as this would be, especially when I'm so attracted to you, I think you're right. Let's take our time and enjoy each other and when that moment comes, we'll know."

"Ok," he says with a smile. He stares at me for a moment not saying anything. I can tell, he feels bad. "I just hope you know that this is not an easy decision at all for me. God Elle; I don't trust myself around you", he says as he leans in and kisses me again lightly. "Especially when you look at me like that, but I want things to be different with us. I really like you." "Aw", I say as I tighten the grip of my legs around him by crossing my ankles. "I really like you too. You're going to have to help me down though because if you don't, I'm just going to keep kissing you and that won't help our case here." He laughs and puts his hands on my hips picking me up and gently plopping me down so that I'm standing next to him once again. I let out an audible sigh and pick up my glass. "Man, I need this sip of wine now more than ever" I say half-jokingly. "Right?" he laughs. "I think we need to do another cheers!" We clink glasses again laughing but holding eye contact as we fill out mouths with the alcohol.

As we're eating dinner, by candlelight might I add, I realize I am having such a great time. The conversation is effortless, without any awkward pauses. I'm learning so much about Ryan that I didn't even know before, and I was married to him! It's like knowing that sex is off the table, for now, has allowed us to be completely transparent with each other. We are talking about topics that took us years to get to before. Maybe it's because Ryan is at a different place in his life this time around, but he's even talking about kids! Kids were never a topic either of us ever discussed before. It was something that we either glossed over or treated it as something we'd get to once we got the restaurant going or once I finished another one of my books. Now though, nothing is off the table. It's so strange to think this but I feel like I'm not reliving my first date again, I'm starting fresh.

"What are your goals, Elle?", he asks me. "Goals?" I repeat as I twirl the pasta on my fork. "Do you mean like long-term or short-term?" "I mean like within the next three or so years; where would you like to be and what would you like to do?" "Hmm", I say as I ponder that question. I haven't asked myself deep questions like that in a long time. "Well, I'm not really sure. I mean, I have always jumped from one relationship to the next and I lived with basically all of them too, so I would first start with having my own place. I also need a job. Writing is wonderful and I'm almost done with my book but I need something that pays the bills too." "You are? That's amazing", he says. "I would love to read it when it's ready, if that's ok with you of course." "Yes, I'd love that," I smile. "I'd love to get your feedback on it."

I hear the record in the living room finish playing music and Ryan asks me if he should put another one on. "Yes, keep it coming" I yell out. I watch him crouch down and scan his records with his pointer finger and smile when he's chosen what he's going to play next. He places the record in and puts the cartridge onto the record and comes back over to where I'm sitting. When the crackling sound starts and the music begins my heart feels like it literally stops. The song that's playing was our first dance song at our wedding. "This song", I whisper out, and then I pause. I have no idea how to finish that sentence. "You like it?" he asks. "Because I actually can't tell what you're thinking." I look over at him and it takes everything in me not to burst into tears. "I love this song", I am able to get out. "Well then", he says as he stands up and puts his hand out for me to grab ahold of, "would you like to dance with me?"

I give him my hand and let him lead me into his living room as I throw my arms around his neck and place my head on his shoulder. We are more so hugging and swaying than dancing but this feels perfect. After a few moments he leans in close to my ear. "I don't know what you're doing to me", he whispers, "but I've never felt this way before. Especially on a first date." Full goosebumps break out just hearing his voice that close to me. "I know", I say into his chest. "I feel the exact same way." I can hear his heart beating faster and faster and I'm breathing right along the same tempo with it. This has to be a sign right; I think to myself. I mean, what are the odds out of his impressive record collection that he chooses the one album that includes the song to play was our first dance wedding song? You can't make that up! We stay close like this for the rest of the song and he then takes my right hand off from around his neck and takes my hand in his. I can feel that his palm is sweaty so I know he's nervous. He's looking at me so deeply and not saying anything. What is he thinking, I wonder. "What are you thinking?" I blurt out.

"I'm actually at a loss for words," he says as he laughs nervously. "I don't know Elle; I definitely do not feel like we only met a few months ago, that's for sure." "No?" I ask as I shake my head. "No", he says back confidently. "I feel like we've known each other for years, it's the weirdest Deja Vous I've ever experienced. Even meeting you in the coffee shop, it just felt like … that wasn't my first time seeing you. Yet, I also feel like I want to know you more, like I can't know enough about you. I probably sound crazy. I'm sorry, I know this is intense for a first date. You're getting out of a recent marriage too and I'm standing here laying it on thick."

I stand on my tippy toes and give him a light kiss on his lips. "This is perfect", I whisper. "I don't deserve this." "What do you mean", he asks with confusion in his eyes. "I mean, you're such an amazing man that has so much to offer. I'm just a screw up" I say as tears start to fall from my eyes and run down my cheeks. I can't hold them back any longer. I start to sob. "Elle, where is this coming from?" He asks with concern. "Why are you crying? You're not a screw up; you're the amazing one!" I can't look up at him, I can't because I know if I do, I'll say something I'll regret. "Elle, what is it? You're really upset", he says as he's now wiping away my tears on each side of my face with his thumbs. I just feel so awful inside. Ryan deserves a good woman. One whose successful, loyal and appreciates him. I had him and I chose someone else. I can't keep pretending that I'm this amazing person he thinks I am. I'm an emotional mess. I turn my head away from him and cover my eyes with my hands. "Look at me", he directs. "Whatever it is, you can tell me. You can tell me anything." I look up at him and before I can think about what I'm doing, the words leave my mouth. "Ryan, I cheated."

Chapter Thirty-Two

There's a few moments of silence and I wonder if I even said it or if it was another moment lost in my head. "Wait, what?" He asks as he moves his hands away from me and takes a step back. "What do you mean you cheated?" I feel the pain start at the bridge of my nose that usually occurs right before I cry, but I will myself to hold it in. Instead, I take a deep breath and sit down on the loveseat near where we were standing. I bring my legs up so that my knees are meeting my elbows as I hug them close. The fire is dying down, literally and figuratively. "Alright so, this has been weighing on me" I say, in between catching my breath. "I know you said you don't trust cheaters and your last relationship ended because of that and so, I feel like you should know that I too am a cheater, well, was a cheater."

He looks over at the fire and proceeds to place more wood into it. It feels like an eternity. I watch his body language looking to gage something out of his cues I know so well. When he turns around, I see it on his face and my heart sinks. He's let down. He's disappointed and he's checked out. I ruined everything. He isn't even making eye contact with me. How did it go from us making out on the kitchen island to this? Why did I say anything?

He takes a seat on the loveseat next to me and I hear him audibly sigh. "Alright, so you cheated while you were dating someone or while you were married", he asks. "Married", I say. Now I'm the one breaking eye contact. "It was the dumbest thing I've ever done and I regret it every single day. I was drunk, which I know doesn't excuse it but it's the truth and I had been going through a tough time in my marriage. I take responsibility because I initiated the kiss and then after when I realized what I had done I bolted. I couldn't believe I let the fantasy blur into reality." I allow myself to look over at him for a quick minute and I immediately wish I didn't. I know he's trying to be open minded but it's written all over his face. Any trust he had for me is now gone and a wall has gone up.

"You hate me now, don't you?" I ask. He looks up at me and I see such innocence in his eyes. "I don't hate you Elle", he says quietly. "Is that all that happened or was there more?" "No that was it," I say quickly. "We kissed, I realized the mistake I made, stopped the kiss and I left."

He nods as he's processing everything. "So, this", he says as he stops midway to clear his throat, "this is ... something for me to think about. I'm glad you told me," he says warmly as we make eye contact for a brief moment. "I mean, if you're going to tell me, now is as good a time as any. It's just a lot for me because of my last relationship."

"I know", I say as the tears start to form. "I had to tell you, it was eating me alive, not saying something. You deserve an honest woman and I wanted you to know my story. I'm sorry!" "Elle", he says as he stands up and crouches down in front of me. He puts his hand on my thighs and is at eye level but I can't look at him; I'm disgusted with myself. "You don't owe me an apology", he says. "I hope you told Josh though because he deserves to know. Does he know?"

I shake my head no. "Well, you should tell him," he says flatly. I look into his eyes then. God, he is so beautiful. "Would you want to know?" I ask, afraid to hear the answer. "I mean, it happened to you once before. Are you glad you found out or do you almost wish you never found out?" "Am I glad?", He asks as his voices rises slightly. "No, it ripped me apart. It was one of the worst days of my life because it's an ultimate betrayal that I never saw coming but it was also a very different story. It wasn't a one-time thing for her. I mean she was basically having another relationship. I'm glad it came out though because otherwise I'd look like a real idiot, living a lie and not even knowing it." He doesn't know how hard this hits me. He can't know. I would look insane if I told him yeah actually, I meant I cheated on you, when we were married, oh yeah, we were married, you didn't know? So, if he thinks I cheated on Josh then so be it. At least we can talk semi freely about this.

"I don't know what to say", I tell him. He's still crouched down with his hands on me. "I'm just sorry that you see that I'm the type of person who was capable of doing this. I understand if it taints your vision of me and who you thought I was. I also understand if you don't want to pursue anything, because it's baggage and you deserve someone who knows how wonderful you really are and who would never disrespect you in that way." "Well, thank you", he says with a little smile. "I do think you're being a tad self-deprecating though. Scoot over", he orders as he sits down next to me and in one swift motion lifts me to sit on his lap. I just collapse into his arms and cry into his chest that I was just moments ago laying my head on in a totally different scenario. "Well, this isn't typically how my first dates go", he says flatly and this makes me laugh. I laugh and cry onto him for a minute. Something in me makes me look up at him and when I do, I give him a hard, good kiss. For a moment we get swept away and it gets heavy. He's kissing my neck as I'm slowly unbuttoning his shirt. I hear him groan and he grabs my face and kisses me back just as hard as he scrambles at pulling my cardigan off of my shoulder. Just as quickly as the kiss started, he pushes his head back and stops it. "Remember the rule?" He asks. "Yeah", I say with a half-smile. "I do. I can see he looks ashamed; already breaking too many rules with me. I'm a wild card. "I should actually go", I say. "I mean, this has been a wonderful time but I think I've displayed enough emotions in your space for one night."

"Yeah, that's probably a good idea" he says back and again my heart sinks.

"I have a lot of thinking to do and process because, yeah", he pauses. "Same thing, lots of emotions for one night. I'll go get your purse." He taps his hand on my thigh as a signal for me to get off of him and it's a slightly awkward movement of me trying to move out of the way. As he's getting my things my eyes scan around his house thinking, will I ever be back here? Is this it? Did I ruin my second attempt with Ryan? He comes back out with my purse and hands it to me as I put it over my shoulder as quickly as I can. "Alright well", I say, "ummm talk to you later?" "Yeah, I'll call you Elle", he says as he gives me a hug but it feels like a space is now between us and he literally taps my back with his hands. That's the kiss of death right there, I think. I try to linger in the moment and grasp on to his hand and hold it for a minute. We look at each other and I just don't want to leave but I know I have to. My hand is trailing up his wrist touching the skin underneath his watch and it's like I want to touch every part of him that isn't exposed. Every part of his skin that's "forbidden", that others don't get to see. "Elle", he whispers. I know if I tried hard enough, I could get him to bring me to his room, but that's not fair to him. "Ok, right, I'll see you later" I say as I turn around and walk away. I half hope he'll come after me and bring me back in but instead I hear the sound of the door close behind me.

I head back to Gwen's and see the lights are all off. It's almost midnight so it makes sense that she and her family would be sleeping. I sit in my car for a moment and let myself wail. I give myself permission to feel sorry for the life of mine that's gone, feel guilty for what I did to end the life I knew and loved and feel the lightness of finally getting out what I did to the person I did it to, even if he didn't know. After I collect myself, I head into the house.

I close the door as quietly as I can without it making any loud noises and walk on my tiptoes to the guest bedroom. I plop myself down on the bed and find I still have my bottle of Merlot I had while I was getting ready for the date. That feels like a lifetime ago. I open the bottle and instead of pouring it in a glass I just drink straight from the bottle. As I'm glugging the wine and letting the vinegary taste hit the back of my throat the door opens. It's Gwen. She looks at me and I look at her and my lower lip trembles and I start to cry. She comes over to sit on the bed and gives me a quick hug before asking me what happened. I give her a brief synopsis and as I'm finishing the part where we had our last kiss she's already picking out and changing into my clothes and putting her hair up. "Wait, what's going on?" I ask. "Get up, she says. "We're getting out of here. It's what, 12:20", she confirms as she looks at my phone. "We've got a solid hour and a half, we're going out."

We're sitting at the bar at the pub nearby and it's pretty clear that I'm getting hammered. "It's over Gwen," I say loudly as I take a shot of tequila. "Over!! Finito! Finished! Donezo!" "If you say one more word to signify the meaning of done, I'm going to hit you" she says close to my face. I wait a few beats and then say, "Terminated!" She smacks me on the arm, "knock it off. You're a shot away from me leaving you here." "You would never!" I slur out to her. "You're right I wouldn't, just lower your tone." "Ok, ok, I'm sorry. God, I'm apologizing to everyone tonight" I say as I start to feel teary eyed again. "I just love him so much. I fell back in love with him all over again and saw things that I neglected in the past. I really effed up, several times." "Alright, can I talk now?" She asks. "Shoot", I say. "You shoot as I take a shot." I take the next shot that's lined up for me. "Ok, did you eff up before when you kissed Josh? Sure, that was an eff up. You're human Elle. Sorry to break it to you but that's a human reaction to feeling many things that were layering on top of you over and over and over until you felt so heavy and hot you just had to pull the damn blanket off of you."

I look at her in amazement. "What?" She asks. "You're like Socrates," I say. "Eh, I don't know if that's really that fitting of an assessment" she laughs but I cut her off. "No, I mean you're so wise and right. It just kept hitting me and hitting me and I felt stifled. My whole body felt itchy, like I needed to crawl out of my skin and run. I didn't vocalize it to anyone. I just looked for an outlet and there Josh was. That bastard!" I yell out a little too loudly as I take back another shot. "And then", I say as I wipe the trickle of tequila that missed my mouth, "and then I hurt my beautiful, beautiful husband and then … then I get another chance with him. I mean who gets that? I did, and surprise surprise; I ruined it."

"Alright so", Gwen says as she rolls up her sleeves. "I think you're being too harsh on yourself. I don't really think you ruined it. I mean you were extremely honest with him. You didn't have to tell him anything but you felt like in order to have any kind of chance of an honest go around you had to tell him so you did. I also don't really think that he took it that badly. It doesn't seem to sound like he's going to ghost you Elle." "I don't know Gwen; you didn't see it. You didn't see him retreat; you didn't see the look in his eyes. I probably looked desperate too just trying to kiss him still and seduce him into what? Sleeping with me and forgetting everything? Even after he said he wanted to take it slow? I'm a terrible person." I put my hands in the bowl of nuts in front of me and then let them fall back in slowly as if they were sand in an hourglass.

"Alright, can we change subjects here for a second" she asks as she smacks my hand away from the nuts. "How was the chemistry before you told him something a past version of you did?" "Oh my God" I swoon. "Gwen, it was like every molecule of my being was turned on. I've slept with him before; I've been intimate with him before but this was so different. I don't know; I want to text him, should I text him?" I ask as I take out my phone. "Nope, nope" she says as she grabs my phone from me. "You'll thank me for this tomorrow, trust me."

The conversation goes back and forth between very heightened emotions and I get to a point of being so drunk where I actually lay my head down on the bar. "Alright, and that's our cue", Gwen says as she signals the bartender for her tab to be closed out. I make my way off of the barstool and as I'm walking to the door, I know it's not going to be good. Things are swaying and my vision is slightly blurry. I open the door and the cool air does help a little bit but not enough. I take a few deep breaths but I still feel that familiar puckering feeling happening to my cheeks. "You're going to get sick aren't you?" she asks. "Oh, hell yeah" I manage to get out before I get into a squatting position. I'm on the side of the parking lot throwing up as she's holding my hair back. "I suck" I say in between getting sick "and you, you're such a good friend" I say looking at her lovingly. "Mm hmm thanks" she says as she's looking the other way waiting for this to pass. After this, everything in my head goes dark.

Chapter Thirty-Three

I wake up and realize immediately I'm not in my room, or the room I've been staying in at Gwen's I should say. My neck hurts like it was slept on strangely and as the room starts to unfold in front of my fuzzy haze I realize I'm on the couch in Gwen's living room. It's like a movie reel of memories starts to flood my brain and it's going so fast it's making me unsteady and nauseous. Date with Ryan, making out on the kitchen island, dancing … dancing to OUR wedding song, tears, me telling him I cheated, me leaving, bar with Gwen, tequila, shots, cry, shots, screaming we're done, tears again, throwing up, drive back where I sing out loud and cry in between words and that's it. Ew, I think as my head is pounding and my throat is bone dry it's scratchy but I feel too weak to even sit up let alone get up.

"You need coffee?" I hear Gwen say. She sounds like she's miles away but when I allow my eyes to focus, I realize she's actually pretty close to me. "Wha …?" I start to say back to her, but can't finish a single word. "Yeah, you definitely need coffee", she smiles. I close my eyes until she's back in front of me with an oversized coffee mug and a plate with toast on it. "I'm not going to eat that." I say to her as I slowly sit up and grab the coffee. "I know you don't want to, but you're going to", she demands as she places the plate on my lap and walks back into the kitchen. "I must have been pretty bad if I didn't even make it to my bedroom," I say with a hoarse voice. "What did you say?" Gwen asks me with a confused tone. "I said, ah I must have been bad last night." I can't even get the rest of the sentence out without feeling sick to my stomach. "Yeah, you were, but it's ok I held your hair back for you."

Gwen walks back into the living room and is sitting next to me looking at me with sympathy. "What?" I ask. "How are you doing?" She asks slowly. "I mean really." "I've been better", I reply with a sarcastic laugh as I take a bite of the dry bread and drink my coffee. The coffee actually does taste really good right now and I'm slowly starting to feel like a person again. "I know I was a hot mess last night and I'm sorry. You've been so great to me and have been there for me when you didn't have to be; I mean you have your own family and your own issues." "Stop", she cuts me off. "This isn't about me. How is Elle? You went through a lot last night and before we get interrupted, I just want to check in with you." Oh, right, I think. Greg and the kids must be on their way back from spending time at his parents' house. "I don't know how I am to be honest. I just feel like such a terrible person and I know it's complicated but I do feel guilty. I just think I ruined things with Ryan. Kissing Josh was a huge mistake and I wish it never happened." "Well, I don't think you ruined things with Ryan," Gwen says as she pats my knee. "Yeah, Josh sucks though, agreed. You just don't seem like you're happy though, you haven't for a little while if I'm being honest with you. Could be why this happened to begin with." "Well, yeah I think, that's all true. I'll be right back", I announce. "If we're going to continue talking, I need to wash my face and brush my teeth", I laugh as I slowly get myself up and walk into the bathroom.

I hear Gwen say something but I can't make it out. I'll ask when I come back out. As I'm washing my face and letting the warm water hit my skin, I hear the doorbell ring. I wonder who that is. I hear Gwen say warmly, "Hey, come on in." I dry my face with a nearby towel and notice something strange. Where's my toothbrush, I wonder. It's not here. I look to see if it fell on the floor, but I see nothing. "That's odd", I say out loud looking at my face in the mirror. "Elle", Gwen is yelling, "your hubby's here!" What? My mind screams. Why would Josh be here? Why is she calling him my hubby and why is she being so nice to him? She literally just said he sucks. I'm so confused and I also don't want to come out of this bathroom. I take a moment to assess my reflection looking back. My face looks pale, skin looks dry and also blotchy. My eyes look bloodshot and my hair looks flat. In a word, I look wretched. I use my fingers to brush my hair out and then try to fluff it to give the appearance of volume. The face and eyes, well there's nothing I can do there so Josh will just see what he sees and deal with it. I wonder why he's even here. To try to get me back? There's no way that's happening at all. I can't believe Gwen would let him in and not give me a warning. I take three deep breaths in and three deep breaths out and tell myself ok girl, it's now or never.

I open the door and as I'm walking down her long hallway, I hear laughter. They're laughing! What is happening? As I make the right turn to enter the living room my heart stops and I freeze. It's not Josh that's standing here with Gwen laughing, it's Ryan. I literally can't move or speak. I'm just standing about ten feet away from them staring. Gwen looks up at me and gives me a look like, "play it cool!" and then Ryan slowly turns around. When his eyes meet mine, I have a moment of confusion. Something seems off. His face looks different to me and his eyes look so warm and inviting, like last night never happened. Then he opens his mouth and says it. "Oh, sweet pear, you look like you had a rough night!"

Chapter Thirty-Four

What in the actual, what? I think. Ryan doesn't call me that name. I mean, he did but not this Ryan. I also look and notice that he has a wedding ring on his finger. Our wedding ring. I look at my finger and notice there's not one on mine. "If you're looking for your ring, I put it with all of your other jewelry before you collapsed onto the couch last night," Gwen laughs. "Hang on, I'll go get it." "I'll come with you", I shout quickly as I follow her down the hallway. I walk behind her, push her into her room and close the door behind us. "What is wrong with you?" She asks. "You're being totally obvious and Ryan is going to catch on." "Catch onto what", I ask in the lowest decimal possible while getting very close to her face. She stares at me not moving back an inch and says, "ok do you have a concussion or something? You do remember what happened last night, right? We were literally just talking about it!"

I take a moment and think. This could be one out of two options. Option number one; I had a date with Ryan just as I remember and we went to a bar where I thought I ruined my chances by telling him I cheated. Option number two, is that we are now back into the other life and my last night then would be.... the kiss with Josh.

I mull over these options for a moment and Gwen looks at me like I really am crazy. We sit in silence not breaking eye contact until I decide to roll the dice and go with my gut. "I kissed Josh", I whisper. "Yeah, you did", she whispers back. "Last night ... I kissed Josh", I clarify. "Correct again", she says. "Also, I'm married, like officially legally married to Ryan", I say slowly. "He's here at your house picking me up, why?" Gwen takes a moment and sits on the edge of her bed holding my jewelry in her hands. "Alright, first I would just like to acknowledge this feels weird but I will go along with it for you. Last night we went to a bar, all of us girls, and you ran into Josh and you kissed him. I ran outside to console you because you were obviously upset and you told me what you did and then threw up. None of us had our cars last night but I had your phone because you gave it to me. Your husband, Ryan, was calling you so I was giving him updates on how you were doing and told him it would probably be best if he just picked you up today because I assumed you'd be too hungover to drive home."

"Holy crap, I did it", I say to myself out loud as I plop down on her vanity chair. "I'm married to Ryan again." "Again?" She repeats. "Ok, I am sooo confused!" "I know, I know. Alright, I promise I will explain everything", I say as I'm laughing. "I'll call you the moment I have a second to myself but right now, I want to go in there and love on my husband." I grab the necklaces and earrings she has in her hands and put them in my pocket and place the wedding rings back on my ring finger. I feel like I can't get to him fast enough and am practically sprinting down the hallway to find him sitting at the dining room table on his phone. I walk up to him and he looks up at me and starts to ask, "what is" ... as I throw my arms around his neck and give him the tightest squeeze. "What is this for?" He asks as he puts his phone down and places his arms around my waist bringing me even closer to him. "I just missed you," I say into his ear. "You have no idea how much." "Wow, sweet pear, you need to go out with your friends more often if this is the greeting I'll get", he laughs. As I pull my head back I see his dimple appear. I put my finger on it and gently stroke it while looking into his eyes. "I just want you to know", I say slowly and meaningfully, "that you are such an incredible person. I'm sorry if it seemed I had forgotten that at all." He looks surprised for a moment and then it's replaced with love. "Well thank you beautiful", he says as he puts his hand on my chin and brings me in to kiss him. "I actually needed to hear that", he says warmly. I want to bring him back to me and continue kissing him but this isn't really the place to be going to town on my husband with Gwen standing in the kitchen drinking her coffee. "So uh, where's Greg and the kids?" Ryan asks as we both get up off of the chair and walk over to where she's standing. "Oh, they're at his parents," she smiles. "They'll be back tomorrow." "Uh oh" he says as he grabs my coat and places it on me. "Single woman for the night! Don't do anything wild" he laughs as he gives her a kiss on the cheek and hugs her goodbye. She laughs, a little too forced but he doesn't seem to notice. "No, No I won't be doing anything wild don't worry." As he turns his back away, I look at her and she motions for me to text her later. I will! I mouth to her as I shush her away with my hand and turn to walk out the door. It's also not lost on me that her family is at Greg's parents just like they were for New Year's Eve but my brain hurts too much to try to figure that one out.

The moment we step outside it becomes real. I'm walking with Ryan, my husband, to his car. We're going back to our old house and our old life and the other life is just gone. The sun is shining in my eyes and I don't know if it's the hangover coming back or the fact that I literally jumped back into my lifetime but I feel dizzy. He notices something is off when I'm not standing next to him and turns around to grab me before I fall. "Hey", he says as he's looking into my eyes. "You ok?" "Yeah, it's just, I think, I'm not feeling well." "Alright, let me get you into the car," he says concerned as he has his arm around me so gently but also with power. It makes me realize how he's always had my back. He's always been my safety net and protector. He's always been there for me; but I haven't been there the same for him. God, will this guilt ever go away?

I'm riding in the passenger side as he's driving us home and I'm lost in my head looking out the window. I don't feel like I'm really here and I don't feel like he's next to me; it's so bizarre. I had envisioned this moment for months and now that I'm here I feel like I want to press pause. "Are you doing ok?" He asks with caution as he places his right hand on my knee. Just like that, I feel it. The electricity. It's still here; it didn't leave and stay with the other life. This makes me so incredibly happy and I interlock my fingers with his and take in an audible sigh of relief. "I'm feeling much better," I say with a smile. He looks confused but also happy. "Ok good because you had me worried there for a moment. You looked like you were going to pass out." "I know but now I'm ok", I say. "I've just been doing a lot of thinking Ryan. About our life and our futures and I think that I haven't been that supportive of you and your dream to open your own restaurant. I'm sorry and I want you to know that I believe in you. I can seriously envision how successful you'll be." "I know you do, Sweet pear", he says as he brings my hand up to his lips and gives it a light, sweet kiss. "I know you do. I haven't been in the best mood either and I know that's affected you and us too. I've been really stressed out and overwhelmed and so I just want to remove myself and get my own space when I get like that."

"No, I've pushed you away", I say forcefully. "I've projected all of my emotions onto you and have also been resentful of you and of the time you've been spending working on your business and that's not fair of me. You can do amazing things Ryan. I know it. You're going to go really far and be successful and I never want you to feel I'm judging you or that I'm holding you back", I say quietly. "Holding me back?" He asks as he lets go of my hand. "Why would you think that? You don't hold me back Elle."

We sit in silence for a few minutes and I have so many thoughts swirling through my head. I obviously held him back in some capacity because in a world without me he was very successful. I remember hearing about the butterfly effect and how one different route can alter everything and it seems to me that I was that change. He didn't have to worry about my needs and worry about basically funding both of us when I was between my books. I can't help but feel like dead weight in some ways. Then I go and repay him by kissing an ex-boyfriend

We are pulling into our driveway and I feel my heart beating and a cold sweat is starting to form. No, no no no no I repeat in my head. Push it away, just relax and breathe. Ryan presses the button to open the garage and he drives the car in and turns it off. He's unbuckling his seatbelt and is opening the door when I place my hand on his arm to stop him. I can't look at him. I'm looking straight ahead and I feel like I'm going to be sick. "Elle, what is it?" He asks with concern. "You're not acting like yourself at all. All this talk about holding me back and telling me how amazing I am, it's almost like..." he pauses. We sit in silence for a minute. "It's almost like what, Ryan?" I ask. "It's almost like you're saying good bye or something, which makes no sense at all. Right?" There's a beat of silence. I can't will myself to speak. "Elle, whatever it is, you can tell me. You can tell me anything." That's my cue and I know it. I feel him looking at me and I can take on his worry as if it's my own. For him this has to be coming out of left field and it's not right to keep him in this limbo.

I allow myself to turn my head and look over at him. His eyes. His eyes look so innocent, sad, vulnerable, confused. He knows something big is about to happen but doesn't know what it is. I do. Am I ready to do this? Everything in my life will change when I do, I know this. It's like something in my mind just won't let me move on if I don't. It will eat away at me, day after day like a parasite. Every moment we share, every morning at breakfast when he asks me to pass the butter, I will feel it in my stomach. Guilt. But now, there's something else. It's a feeling that no matter what he says to me, I feel he may be more without me. I've seen that other side. Even though I know, through all of that, through all of his success, somehow, he was still interested in me.

He still saw something in me he wanted, desired. Technically, I did the confession already. So why can't I just tell myself that? It's already been done, Elle. Let it go. Move forward. Don't hurt him anymore just because you feel this will "clear the air" if you do. That's selfish really, isn't it? Isn't that what people say when they confess? They only confessed because it made them feel guilty and that's selfish?

I know my mind is spiraling and truth be told, I have no idea what to do. I just know now I have started something that I can't go back on. I saw it in his eyes. He knows I need to tell him something important, something potentially life changing. I can't pretend it was something silly. I need to just pull it together and speak.

I hear him repeating my name, and I don't know how long he's been saying it for. I just hear the tone has changed and there's a brokenness in the sound. The sound of hearing him say Elle has changed. It's time.

I clear my throat as I face him and say, "Ryan, I have to tell you something."

Acknowledgements

First and foremost, this book literally wouldn't have happened if it weren't for my daughter Mila taking her glorious 3 hour naps a day. In a world of quarantine, writing became my guilty pleasure. My time for just me where I could indulge and imagine a world outside of being couped up in my home raising a 10-month-old during a pandemic! I thank you Mila for showing me your magic and providing me with endless entertainment. I hope when you get older you read and adore this book as much as I've loved writing it. Never forget that you are complete as you are and everyone else in your life is simply a beautiful addition.

To my girlfriends Laura and Erika: thank you for being my first beta readers, even when I only sent you paragraphs at a time. Your enthusiasm and encouragement for my writing has been so inspiring. I love you girls.

To Andrew, thank you for always supporting me, even when you heard the main character of this book is...well...doing what she's doing. You inspired the term, "Sweet Pea" as that was your first nickname for our daughter.

To my mom for never giving me a limit on how many books I could take out as child at the library. My adoration of books starts with you!

To anyone else I may have forgotten. Anyone in my life that has shown an interest, asked me questions about this book along the way or has told me they can't wait to read it. You kept me going! Thank you.

Made in the USA
Middletown, DE
09 December 2022